Just ONE

C.E. JOHNSON

Want to stay up to date on all important announcements and new releases?
** Sign up for my newsletter! **

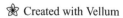 Created with Vellum

JUST ONE

IN THE DARK #2

C.E. JOHNSON

DEDICATION

For my mom. The strongest woman I know.

MESSAGE TO READERS

This story mentions mental illness and suicide. If you or a loved one are struggling with depression or thoughts of suicide, please call the National Suicide Prevention Lifeline 1-800-273-8255.

CHAPTER ONE

"I WISH you didn't have to leave."

My brother's voice carries the sadness we both feel. Picking up my phone from the side table, my eyes dart quickly to the empty place where the lamp once sat. The lamp that's now in a million pieces in the trash along with numerous other broken items. I'm more worried now about leaving than I ever have been before.

"I have to go back to work, Jarrod. Pretty soon Finn is going to fire my ass. There aren't too many bosses who give their employees the amount of time off that he's given me."

My boss, Finnegan O'Reilly, is the owner of O'Reilly's Pub. He's been really great about giving me time off when I need it. I know it leaves him short staffed, so it's important I get back to work. I straighten the couch pillows I bought Jarrod when he moved into this place. As if perfecting them is going to change the heaviness in the room or the way I feel about leaving.

"C'mon, Daphne. Why do you care about that shitty pub job anyway?" Jarrod asks, annoyed. "The money Gram left us covers your rent just fine."

"Working at O'Reilly's is fun and it keeps my mind off shit."

"You mean my shit." Jarrod angles his head toward the ground with guilt.

"Don't you dare go there."

Moving close to him, I put my hands on my older brother's tall shoulders. "I wouldn't trade you or my time with you for anything in the entire world. It has nothing to do with you. We both know I have my own issues."

"I know," he says.

Relief flows through me, thankful he didn't take that the wrong way and spin out of control right before I'm supposed to leave. Three weeks have already passed since I arrived at Jarrod's house. I need to get back to Boston, back to work, and back to life.

"You know I don't want to leave you. If you would have moved to Boston with me, we would both be saving ourselves a load of trouble."

Jarrod rolls his eyes. "Oh, sure. Following my sister around would be awesome."

Moving slowly, I grab my things from around the room and begin to pile them by the front door. Coming back to Albany is tough. It's home, but it's also the root of many of my problems. I miss Jarrod when I'm in Boston, but it's usually not a great time when I come back here.

My brother has had a lifetime of internal pain to rival almost anyone. The demons that live within him have crushed many dreams he's had. Many that I've had. We've struggled for so long to find the right medications and the right dosage to ease his symptoms, but nothing's worked perfectly.

Life has always been about Jarrod. My childhood was nonexistent. There were no fun playdates or tea parties. I can't remember a single instance of my mother taking us to the park or to a movie. Mom was always going out to events and parties to keep up her social elitism. She dragged Daddy with her. They would be gone for days. The nannies they hired tried so hard to help Jarrod, but I seemed to be the only one who knew how to handle him during his episodes. They had me helping him way before my mind was ever ready, and it affected other aspects of my life.

The girls at school would invite everyone but me to their sleepovers. Their whispers were loud. I'm not sure I would have gone even if I were invited. The thought of Jarrod being alone stopped me from doing most things without him. I never took that out on him, though. It wasn't his fault.

Now, Jarrod lives about fifteen minutes from our parents' estate. He wanted to feel independent but the thought of buying a home on his own gave him anxiety, so we bought it together. I thought having a home relatively close to our parents would encourage them to visit. I was wrong. My mother would call me but only to check on Jarrod. She never asked about me or how I was doing. My mother and I haven't always seen eye to eye. I never understood the life she lived and she never understood mine. I know she loves me only because it's her job as a mother to do so. I also know, she loves Jarrod more. Once Jarrod was discussed, she'd turn the conversation to her and their constant dinners with their rich friends. She would tell me she loved me, even though it always sounded forced, and then I wouldn't hear from her for weeks. Even though it shouldn't have, it hurt when my mother quit calling me altogether. She gets all of her information from Ryan now.

Ryan and Jarrod have been best friends since kindergarten and he's a big part of our family. He moved in with Jarrod when I moved out. Ryan has learned how to help Jarrod with his doctor appointments and his medications. I never would have been able to move to Boston had it not been for him.

I don't know what's going to happen when Ryan moves out. It's bound to happen. He's had a serious girlfriend for over a year now. I can't imagine he's going to ask her to move in with his bipolar best friend.

"Are you sure that you're feeling better?" I ask, eyeing Jarrod closely.

He nods. "I have an appointment with Dr. Hammond first thing in the morning. I'm much better. I promise."

Ugh. I wish he would stop promising anything. We both know that he doesn't have control over himself sometimes. Promises are about as good as already chewed-up gum.

I turn to the mirror by the front door, and twist my long ash-blond hair up into a messy bun. I place my oversized sunglasses on my face in attempt to hide my worried eyes. At a snail's pace, I grab my sweater off of the back of the couch next to the large window in Jarrod's living room. The sun is shining brightly outside and the flowers of spring have started to bloom, but there is still just a bit of a chill in the May air.

"It's a beautiful day. Maybe we should go for lunch before I leave. Are you hungry? I'm kind of hungry."

"Daphs, you're stalling. I'm going to be fine. Not like I want you to go, but I also don't want you driving home in the dark."

Jarrod knows that if we go to lunch, I'll delay even more with something else for us to do and it would be night before I got home. The drive back to Boston takes a little under three hours depending on traffic. When the chance came up for me to move to Boston, I jumped. There was so much hope inside me, that Boston would change my life. Sadly, I still can't seem to make my life my own, even from three hours away.

"Love you, Brother. I'll call you as soon as I get home." My arms wrap around his torso and squeeze him tightly. As always, I deeply inhale the clean cotton scent of Jarrod's clothing. My finger taps on the yellow sun that adorns the front of his favorite black sweatshirt like I do every time he has it on. I bought him the sweatshirt years ago. I told him when he puts it on the sun is always shining even on the cloudiest of days. The tap is reminder not just for him, but also for me.

"I love you, too," he says. He squeezes me back and places a kiss on the top of my head. "Now get. I want you home before dark. Call me the second you walk into your apartment."

I grab my things by the door, turn to Jarrod, and study him for a moment. Sometimes siblings don't even look like they come from the same family. Then there are siblings like Jarrod and me. Other than the height difference, we look as though we could be twins. Both with ash-blond hair, blue eyes, and rounded facial features. We exchange our identical wide smiles, then I walk out of the house.

* * *

THREE HOURS LATER, I pull into my ridiculously overpriced parking spot in a garage across the street from my apartment. I grab as much as I can carry and decide to leave the rest in the car for tomorrow. My arms feel like they are breaking off as I struggle to get my key into my door.

"Let me do it."

A smile breaks out over my face as my neighbor and best friend, Leigh, grabs the key from my hand and opens my door. Meowing immediately rings loudly through the apartment. Stopping just inside the entry, I drop everything in my hands and sit on the floor. The ball of onyx fur crawls onto my lap and starts to purr.

"Herman, I've missed the hell out of you. Was Leigh nice to you? Did she feed you all the treats she was supposed to?"

"Of course I did. He likes me better than you anyway," Leigh says with a smirk. She makes her way into my living room and plops herself down on the couch.

Every time I come back, I remember why I left Albany. Walking through my front door always feels like home. I've worked hard to make this space cozy and warm retreat. I searched for months for the perfect couch and it's my favorite piece in the open floor plan of my tiny apartment. The black velvety sectional floats in the combined living and dining area. I've adorned it with about a hundred squishy light gray pillows and soft throw blankets. There's a two-person table against the wall behind the couch. I have an inconceivable amount of candles that sit in rose gold holders peppered all around the open space. Between the couch and dining table is a skinny door to a miniscule balcony with only enough room for one chair and a potted plant. But it's still a balcony. Still sitting at the front door, I look to my right to see my mail piled up on the kitchen counter. Giving Herman a kiss on the top of his head, I place him to the side and go to flip through the stack.

"How's your brother?"

"He's doing okay. It was rough when I got there. Broke damn near everything in sight. It got a little scary. Hopefully the meds they have him on now will actually work. Thanks for watching Herman again."

"Always. So what do you want to do tonight? Chinese?"

"Have I ever said no to Chinese?"

"Nope, and neither have I," she giggles.

Leigh and I clicked the first day I moved into this apartment. She came over to introduce herself and ended up staying for two hours chatting. She's the best friend I've ever had. Hell, she's the only friend I've ever had. We've gotten into the same habit every time I get back from Jarrod's house. She'll ask how he is, and then doesn't bring it up again because she knows that I am usually completely exhausted by the time I make it back home.

After picking up my stuff from the front door of my apartment, I walk to the hallway across from the kitchen and toss everything down in front of the laundry closet. I reach into my purse and grab out my phone to see five missed calls from Jarrod. He watches the clock as soon as I leave and if I don't call him right when I should be home, he starts blowing up my phone. I scroll to his name and press it.

"Are you home now?" he greets, sounding worried.

"Yes. I'm home. Leigh and I are just about to order Chinese."

"Good. I'll talk to you tomorrow?" he asks.

"You know you will. Love you."

"Love you too, Daphs."

Leigh and I watch shit reality TV as I devour my Kung Pao Chicken. These shows always have a way to make us feel better about our own fucked up lives. After we polish off a pint of ice cream, she heads back to her apartment next door where her husband and two-year-old son are sleeping.

I shower off the last three weeks, then climb into bed where I lay for an hour listening to the clothes tumbling in the dryer. I can't sleep. Too many thoughts run circles around my head. This time was scary with Jarrod. He was manic when I got there and dreadfully irrational. Of all the years my brother has been fighting this illness, he's never once put his hands on me. This time, he pushed me so damn hard, I fell backwards onto my ass. It wasn't long after, his mood began to change and he fell into his depressive state. For days, I could barely get him to leave his bed. He gets on medication that seems to work for a while, but it gradually stops working and his psychiatrist tries something else. It's a constant battle, which takes so much of my time. Time that I'm supposed to be at work.

I'm lucky to have a boss like Finn. Not only is he a fine hunk of sex to look at, he lets me take off whenever I need to and asks no questions. There's just one issue with Finn. Last year, Finn and I had sex. Twice. I'm just not sure how it happened. We went into his office to talk about my schedule, and before I knew it, my ass was on his desk. About a month later, we had a discussion in his office about a company policy discouraging relationships between employees. We agreed not to do it again and shook hands, except our hands held onto each other a little longer than they should have. That's when the second time happened.

Neither of us even undressed.

That was it though. It had to stop. There's just no time for any kind of relationship that requires commitment. I'm gone so much and incapable of putting anyone else first, including myself. If only things were different. I think about Finn every night and what it could be like to have a real relationship with a guy like him. A girl can dream.

My phone says that it's shut-your-fucking-eyes-already o'clock. I turn on the TV, flip to my stomach, and close my eyes. This may seem counterproductive to some. For me, the quiet is disturbing. Silence is painful. If I want any sleep at all, I need the sound of the TV to drown out my own troubled thoughts.

* * *

THE PHONE RINGS, 9 AM on the dot. Every day, no matter what.

"Hey, Bro," I answer, my voice hoarse.

"Wake up! The sun is shining."

"I wouldn't know, I have room-darkening curtains. I work nights, remember?" I say, giving Jarrod a hard time. Ever since I moved to Boston alone, he calls me every morning at the same time. He worries about me working at the pub so late at night. It's become a comfortable habit for Jarrod. When I think about it, I need his phone call just as much as he needs me to pick up the phone.

"All right, I'll let you get back to sleep."

"Okay. Love you."

"Love you, too."

Knowing that I have to wake up to get ready for work in a couple of hours, I cover my head up with the blankets and go back to sleep.

* * *

My bowl is filled to the brim and I do a balancing act so I don't dump my favorite cereal all over my floor on the way to the couch. I'm sure this has something to do with the extra junk in this trunk, but I could care less. I would give anything for a big bowl of cinnamon and sugar squares.

After finishing my cereal, and laughing at the rich women on TV arguing about whose boat they are taking to some island, I freshen up and head to the closet to dress for work. Some might say that I don't fit the typical mold like the rest of the staff at O'Reilly's. My style is just a bit different than theirs. Over half of the staff is early twenty-year-olds working their way through college. Most of the girls dress more feminine and wear super tight, low-cut shirts for heftier tips. It's a sea of baby pink. I'm not knocking their game; I'm just not that type. I'm a jeans and t-shirt kind of girl. Usually, it's some kind of a smart-ass graphic tee. Today I grab my black Jack Daniels tank that is shredded in the back, a pair of ripped jeggings, and my black and white Chucks. I love working at the pub because if I had to dress up every day to go to work, I'd be miserable. My parents forced us to dress up our entire childhood, even if it was just for the nannies.

I was fortunate to be born into a wealthy family. My grandparents left my brother and me enough money to live comfortably for damn near our whole life if we budgeted well. I don't need my job for the financial stability. I need it for the mental stability. The routine itself brings me a little tranquility. Every day, I get dressed, walk to work, do my job, then get greeted by the one man I can count on when I get back home. Herman.

The warm afternoon sun escorts me on my walk to the pub. I don't drive because it would be pointless. I already pay a shit ton of money to park in my garage. It would be stupid to pay again to park it in a different garage while I'm at work. The only reason I even own a car is so I can get to Jarrod.

Tasha looks relieved to see me enter the pub and starts waving wildly in my direction as she bounces to another table with her notepad in hand. This pub also strangely feels like home to me. When I'm gone, I miss it. The dark wood panels on the walls. The smell of ale wafting through the air. O'Reilly's is more than just a regular pub. It has a few booths and tables along with the bar, and we serve lunch and dinner with the traditional Irish stew being one of the top sellers. Kael —Finn's brother—hired Tasha when Sophie left.

Sophie worked here for a long time. She is a tough chick, but you wouldn't know it by the casual conversation with her. She rarely comes into the pub anymore, but when she does, it's a big deal. Sophie could rock this bar. She could have every table in the pub and no one would wait more than a minute for their drinks. Tasha, however, is a mess. She might be able to deliver one beer in a minute, but that's only if she doesn't trip and spill it all over the floor first.

Part of me is relieved that I don't see Finn anywhere. The other part of me trembles at the thought of his eyes meeting mine after being gone and not seeing him for so long.

"Hey, Daphne," I hear come from one of the booths to my right. Kael O'Reilly is sitting in a booth filling out some paperwork. He hates doing the pub's paperwork so I'm surprised to see him in a good mood.

"I see the place is still standing without me."

"Barely. I can't tell you how happy I am that you're back." Just as Kael speaks, we both wince at the sound of a glass breaking. A red-faced Tasha is sweeping up the broken glass. "I'm about out of beer mugs," he chuckles. "Did you have fun?"

If only he knew just how much *fun* I had. I don't talk about Jarrod. Not because I'm embarrassed, but because it's just nobody's business.

I'm protective of him, and if I can ever convince him to move to Boston with me, I don't want people to look at him with a preconceived notion.

"A blast," I say as I flash him a friendly smile.

It's a busy evening, which I'm thankful for. There's nothing worse than coming home from a trip to Albany and having nothing to focus on other than my thoughts and fears. I balance a tray full of fish and chips on one hand, while the other is holding two bottles of beer when Finn appears from the back. He comes closer, captivating me in his usual black O'Reilly's sleeveless shirt.

"Your feet glued to the floor?" he asks me. Snapping out of it, I realize I was staring and had stopped walking. *Damn it.*

"I have a cramp in my calf," I blurt out and start walking again, pretty damn proud of myself that I came up with something so quickly.

Ignoring the prickling of my skin, I deliver the food and beers. I check in on my other tables then head back up to the bar. Finn is leaning against the counter with his arms crossed looking like a mass of man. His eyes are zoned in on me. I bite my lower lip contemplating if I want to ignore him completely or drag him into the back and watch his muscles contract above me. Everything in me wants to do the second, but the smart move is the first.

"Do you have a problem, Finn?" I ask.

"Nope." The word quickly falls out of his mouth.

"Then is there a reason you're staring at me?"

"You have a good time on your trip?" he asks.

He's never asked me that before, and my stomach turns, worried about where this might be headed.

"Yeah, it was all right."

"Good. Need to talk to ya'. Take care of your tables and meet me in the back."

"Finn—"

"I said, I need to talk to ya'," he says. He looks serious as he pushes himself off of the bar and heads back to his office.

Quickly making sure that my tables all have what they need, I ask another waitress to keep an eye on them while I talk to Finn. Hands sweating, I walk to the office door. The look on Finn's face tonight is different. I hope to hell he isn't about to fire me, as this has been one of the longest spans of time that I've needed off. It scares me to think of what I would do with so much down time.

The lump in my throat goes nowhere as I swallow hard before turning the handle to Finn's office. After walking in, instead of him locking the door upon my entry and taking me on the desk like deep down I wish he would, he gestures to the chair across from him. *Shit.* This isn't good.

"Finn, you're freaking me out," I confess as I take a seat across from him. This is incredibly too formal for the two of us.

He says nothing.

Nervously, my eyes travel across his tensed biceps, up to those muscles on either side of his neck, to his squared-off jaw and his ocean blue eyes, then to his short reddish-brown hair. My teeth graze along my lower lip. After a few minutes of silence, he leans back in his chair, eyeing me as he interlaces his long, rough fingers and rests them on his chest.

"Finn, what the hell is going on?"

"First, calm down. I need to clear some shit."

"Okay…" I say, confused.

"I don't know what you're doin' when you go on these mysterious hiatuses. Really, it's none of my business. But, if you got a serious dude, what we do ain't cool. Is it serious?"

"What we *do*? Is it serious?" I stutter, completely caught off guard by his assumption.

"When you called to tell me you were comin' back to work, I heard a male voice in the background. Not like I'm a morally innocent man, but I'm not about us flirtin' around if you're about to marry the guy."

"*Marry?*"

"You a fuckin' parakeet?" he asks, his damn half smirk riling up my insides.

"No, I'm not getting married. I don't have a *dude*," I say with a bit of amusement.

"There's no dude?" he repeats.

Still confused, I shake my head. The sound of the chair hitting the wall behind him makes me flinch. Finn moves around the desk and heads toward the door. The click of the lock and turning of the blinds send my temperature skyrocketing. I fidget in my chair. Finn's heat approaches my back and goosebumps rise on my neck as he gently moves my hair from it with his fingertips. Warm lips graze the center of my nape and my head tilts forward, giving him all of it. Slowly, he moves across the side of my neck before his mouth finds mine. The second our lips join, Finn lifts me out of the chair and tosses me onto the desk. My legs unconsciously and comfortably straddle around his tight core.

"Thank God. I can't fuckin' take it anymore," Finn says, his mouth against my collarbone.

"This isn't what I thought—"

"Need this," he says as his mouth covers mine.

My lips close around his before opening them again, inviting him in. His grip becomes tighter and his fingertips dig into my hips. I feel his erection against the inside of my thigh and my brain snaps back to life. Putting my hand to his chest, I gently push him away. Immediately, I regret the loss of his skin against mine. But I don't want to go back to this. It's taken so much effort for me to stay away from Finn, and this is just going to hurl me back into the battle between my heart and my head. Right as I'm about to explain things to Finn, my phone rings. Bad thoughts invade my head. No one calls me while I'm at work unless there is a problem. Fumbling, I grab my phone from the back pocket of my jeans as fast as I can and see that it's Jarrod.

"Jarrod?" I ask, panicked.

Finn's face changes and I can see hurt in his eyes. He moves quickly away from me and plops himself back into his chair behind his desk.

"Jarrod, are you there? What's the matter? Are you okay?" My rapid-fire questions bring on a hesitant silence from the other end. Finn shifts in the chair, leaning forward and analyzing my expression. Faint sniffles and the hitch of my brother's breath are the only sounds coming from the speaker. My skin freezes, my voice is hard to find, and my heart stops in my chest. "Jarrod. I'm coming. I'll leave right now. Just give me a few hours. Okay? You hear me? I'm coming."

"Sorry." One word. One word he blubbers into the phone before he hangs up. My hand rests over my palpating heart as the room starts spinning. Finn moves fast out of the chair and puts his hands on my hips to assure I'm steady.

"I have to go. I have to go right now. My—" My hands tremble noticeably as I grab Finn's hand off my hip and move toward the door of the office.

"I'm drivin'," he says as he grabs my elbow and moves me quickly from the office and to the front door of the pub.

"Kael, take over, we're out. Don't know when we'll be back. I'll call you," he spits.

"You got it," Kael shouts from the behind the bar.

Finn walks fast and I'm barely breathing. I try to call Jarrod back but get no answer. I call Ryan and, again, no answer. Last resort, I call Mom. Shock, no answer there either. Before I even realize how far we've walked or how we got there, Finn opens the door to his Wrangler and practically puts me in. The sound of the door slamming echoes in my head, and I know what I have to do. I have to. My fingers shake typing the numbers into the phone as I hear Finn get into the driver's side.

"Where we goin'?"

"Albany," I whisper and hit SEND on the phone.

"911, what's your emergency?" the operator asks.

"My brother…"

Finn's head spins in my direction, then just as quickly spins back to look at the road as he picks up speed, dodging through the late evening traffic.

"I need somebody to get to my brother's house in Albany, New York. He suffers from bipolar disorder, and he called me crying and said he was sorry." My voice starts to weaken, so I try to clear my throat to say the words. "I think he may be trying to kill himself."

After the operator asked me a few more questions and I give her my brother's address, she assures me they are on their way and will get there as fast as possible. I hang up with her and keep trying to call Jarrod, Ryan, and my parents. An hour and half after Finn and I left Boston, Ryan finally answers the phone.

"Hey, Daphs." The sound of loud music in the background affirms that he isn't with Jarrod.

"Where are you?"

"Daphne, what's wrong?"

"Get to the house. Now," I tell him and hear a slight gasp. I wish I could say this was the first time Ryan has received a call like this.

"I'm only ten minutes away. I'm leaving now," he says and hangs up.

Even though Ryan is on his way, the sick feeling in the pit of my stomach doesn't fade.

"Is this where you've been goin'?" Finn asks softly.

"Yes."

We don't speak the rest of the way. Numerous times, I try to call Ryan but he doesn't answer. I decide to assume that he is taking care of Jarrod and that's why he isn't picking up his phone.

I think I'm going to throw up as we turn the corner to see a street full of fire trucks, police cars, and one ambulance. Finn barely has the car in park when I throw my door open and run to the sidewalk where people are standing around. I only recognize one.

"Ryan! Where's Jarrod?"

When he looks at me, sorrow and heartache is written all over his face.

"Where the fuck is my brother?" I yell.

"Daph… I… he's…" At his stumbling words, I know.

My brother is dead.

My breath hitches, but no tears fall from my eyes. I slowly back away from Ryan, hoping I can get away before he can hurl the heartbreaking truth at me. I don't want to hear the words. My movement stops abruptly as my back runs into Finn's solid body. He places his hands on my arms to console me. Quickly, I shake him off, move to the side, and continue to back up. Deep in my core, I feel it, but my mind doesn't want to hear it. Suddenly, the words come out of his mouth like a bulldozer to my life.

"Daph, he's gone," his best friend cries. "He hung himself."

"Fuck you. Fuck you, Ryan," I yell.

Ryan's eyes widen as Finn lunges forward to grab my head and bury it into his shoulder. I let him and try to settle my sickened stomach until I hear movement coming from behind me. I wretch out of his arms and turn to the scene Finn was trying to protect me from. The blood that once ran warm through my body turns ice cold as the paramedics push out a gurney with a white blanket covering a body. As they load it into the back of the ambulance, all emotions leave me. I turn away from the scene and walk to Finn's Wrangler, open the door, and get in. I'm not in there for more than a minute before three police officers tap on the window. Finn stands outside of the Wrangler as the police speak to me and take my statement.

Completely exhausted and feeling numb, I stare straight ahead but see nothing but darkness in front of my face. I see no streetlights, no houselights, no stars, no moonlight. The world has gone dark. For some, sorrow is obvious from the outside. For me, it is the silent killer of internal destruction.

The sound of the driver's side door opening and closing echoes in the silence. Finn turns and places his hand on my arm.

"Where can I take you?"

Without blinking or shedding one tear, I spit out, "Boston. Get me the fuck out of here."

CHAPTER TWO

SOME MAY CALL IT SHOCK. I feel like I want to cry and scream, but my body just won't let me. Finn keeps asking if I'm okay but I can't answer him. It's as if the ability to speak was taken from me. The empty feeling in my chest is too overwhelming for words. How can I answer that question even if I could find my voice?

Finn pulls up to my building and remarkably finds a parking spot on the side of the road. Unable to move, I sit in the seat, still looking into the lightless world. Finn comes around, opens my door, and holds onto my arm to help me out.

"Thanks, Finn. I'll pay you back for the gas you used driving there and back."

"Are you kiddin' me?" he asks, while glaring at me in an odd way.

"What?"

"Are you doing okay? I mean, I know you're not okay, but…" His words come out slowly.

"Honestly, I have no idea what I am."

"You seem like you're holdin' back. You don't have to hold back for me. I've got you."

"My brother has been sick for a long time. That's the difference between him and me. He wore all his feelings on his sleeve for the entire world to be a witness. I tend to keep mine to myself. Just because I'm not crying right now doesn't mean my world didn't just collapse into rubble right in front of me."

He shuts the door to his Wrangler and beeps the lock from his key fob. "C'mon."

Holding onto my arm, Finn walks me to the door of my building. Turns out, I need his stability because my legs feel like jelly as I walk. All I feel is frigid emptiness. I manage to open the door to the building, and he holds onto me again as we ascend the stairs up to my apartment. Opening the door to my home, I drop my purse and let my legs give out from under me.

"Daphne?"

Finn's hands go under my arms to lift me off of the floor, but he removes them as soon as my little furry man comes running toward me. I bury my head into Herman and hear Finn shut and lock the door. He slowly squats down next to me and pets Herman. Then he places his hand on the side of my head, and for the first time since I got the call, my eyes turn to meet his. Without a word spoken, Finn gives me his sympathy. Holding onto Herman, Finn helps me rise from the floor and I walk slowly to the couch. He heads into the kitchen and starts nosing through my cabinets.

"What are you looking for?"

"Tea. Isn't that what people usually drink to relax? Got any?"

"Yeah, it's in the cabinet right next to the fridge," I tell him, pointing to the right one. Finn makes two cups of tea and joins me on the couch. He takes one sip and makes a sour face.

"What the fuck did I just drink?" he says to himself quietly.

It makes me laugh. I take a sip of the hot liquid and feel it run down my throat, and then I confide in the man that has secretly had a piece of my heart for years.

"There's a deep, black hole that has taken over the inside of my chest and it hurts worse than anything I've ever known. But I can't seem to let it out. I don't know why. Maybe it's because I want to forget that this night ever happened and pretend my brother is sleeping in the house I left him in. I know my reaction seems weird. It feels weird. So please stop looking at me like I'm nuts. It makes me feel like I am."

"You're not nuts, and I ain't lookin' at you like you are."

"You don't have to sit here with me. You only have five hours until you need to open O'Reilly's, and I'll be okay. You should go home and get some sleep," I tell him, taking another sip of the tea he sweetly made for me.

He picks up his phone and dials a number. "Yep. I'm with Daphne. Can you take care of the pub today and get someone to come in and cover her shift tonight? Neither of us will be in today. I'll call you later. Yeah, yeah, okay. I owe you." Finn playfully rolls his eyes as he hangs up the phone.

"Looks like we both got ourselves a day off. You need it and so do I. I'll crash on the couch if you want me to, but I'm not goin' anywhere." His blue eyes look exhausted, and even though I hate to admit it, I don't want to be alone anyway.

"You can sleep in my bed. I'd feel bad if you slept on the couch. No promises I won't hit or kick you in my sleep though," I tell him.

"You been known to do that?"

"So I've been told."

Something flashes in his eyes as he adjusts himself on the couch. *Is he jealous?*

"Guess I'll take the risk."

Finn's footsteps follow mine as we head to the bedroom. He lifts his shirt over his head and tosses it to the floor. I grab an oversized Def Leppard shirt out of my drawer and head to the bathroom. By the time I finish my nightly routine, Finn is stretched out on the right side of the king size bed. His steady breaths are the only sound in the room. Trying not to wake him, I crawl in gently and turn to my side facing away.

Even though the room has curtains that drown out most of the outside light, the faint light of rising sun changes the room from black to the dark gray they are painted. This room is my favorite room in the entire apartment. I made it dark and romantic with lots of rich dark colors and soft fabrics. The dark grays, blacks, and plums are accented with just a few bright white pillows for contrast. It's the first place I go when I'm looking for some kind of peace. I'm not sure peace is going to find me any time soon, no matter what room I'm in. My eyes squeeze tightly closed, begging myself to sleep. But thoughts of Jarrod don't allow it. How lost he must have been to take his own life. His painful last word—"Sorry"—plays on repeat in my head.

...

SWEATY AND CHOKING FOR AIR, my eyes fly open. For a moment, I'm startled when large arms envelope around me. Finn. His hands move frantically over my chest and neck.

"Nightmare," I say.

He takes a deep breath and his hand falls away from me. I lie back onto my pillow, taking long, slow breaths to get myself together. Finn shoves his arm under me and pulls me into his side. My head rests on his chest. His large bicep holds me in place as his fingers trail up and down my arm. The gentle touch works, and I slowly drift back to sleep to the rhythmic beat of his heart.

My phone ringing on my nightstand wakes both of us up. I reach for it, and my heart sinks when I see who is calling.

"Mother," I answer with sympathy in my voice.

"I can't believe it. My baby," she cries into the phone. "You did it. It's your fault he's gone. If you had stayed in Albany like I told you to, he would still be here. My baby boy would still be here."

I remind myself that my mother is grieving for her son. She's trying to find someone to blame, and if it makes her feel better right now, I'll let her blame me.

"He was just sick. I can't even say that I blame him. Nothing worked, and he just couldn't do it anymore. It wouldn't have mattered if I had been there or not." I knew nothing I said was going to make her feel better.

"I'll never forgive you for leaving him. Don't ever come back here.

You are no longer welcome in my home. Your father and I are taking care of everything, other than that house you insisted on buying with him. As far as I'm concerned, both of my children died last night." The phone disconnects as her words cut like shards of glass slicing through the walls of my chest. Motionless, I stare down at the phone for a few minutes.

"Is there somethin' I can do?" Finn asks, and my body jumps slightly, as I forgot he was even there. By the look of concern on his face, I know he heard my mother yelling on the other end of the phone.

"No," I finally answer.

Finn reaches for me, but I move out of the bed before his hands make contact. I can't handle his gentle touch. Maybe she's right. What if I never moved to Boston and stayed with Jarrod? Maybe he would still be here. I bolt off of the bed and move quickly to the bathroom. Standing under the running shower head, I pray the water washes the heartbreak, hate, and guilt off of me. It doesn't work. But it also doesn't bring the tears. I should be a complete disaster right now. The loss of my brother and my mother's words would send most normal people into a pool of tears that drowns them. And yet here I am, unable to shed one even though it feels as if my soul is withering to nothing.

The smell of bacon wafts in the air just as a groan comes from my stomach. I slide on soft lounge shorts, a sports bra, and a black muscle tank. The kitchen comes more into view the more I open the bedroom door. Finn stands at the stove, rubbing his naked chest with one hand. His other hand is cooking bacon and eggs. It's hard not to stare. I've never had a man cook for me before and much less half naked.

"You got a cramp in your calf again?" he asks. A smile crosses his face as he nods at my legs. Shaking the trance off, it also brings me right back into the hell I'm currently living.

The thought of ever being happy is overwhelming knowing my brother could never find his happiness. I'm reminded of the morning phone call that I didn't receive today, and that I never will again. My head hangs low and my eyes focus on a gouge in the hardwood floor. The spatula clanks against the counter and Finn moves to me. This hug feels different than any kind of affection Finn has shown me in the last two years I've known him. He releases the embrace and moves back one step. His eyes give my face a once over then he returns to the stove.

Finn moves around my kitchen flawlessly. He's run O'Reilly's for so many years now, it doesn't surprise me that he knows how to cook. His bacon and eggs would rival many of the diners here in town.

"Can I ask you something?" he asks as he brings both of our plates to the table.

"Sure."

"What's up with the fifty boxes of cereal in your pantry?" he asks with a chuckle.

"I'm obsessed with cereal. I'd eat it all day if it wouldn't add twenty pounds to my ass."

"What's your favorite thing to eat for dinner?"

I know Finn is just trying to create casual conversation and not focus on my sadness. It's what I used to do with Jarrod, too.

"Cereal. But a close second would probably be a nice juicy steak." I flash him a half smile and he returns the same.

The rest of breakfast was quiet. I clean up the dishes before sitting back down at the island, not knowing how to keep my mind off of my life.

"I don't even know what to do," I say.

"Well, what do you feel like doing?"

"Anything but sitting here and thinking."

Suddenly, three knocks come from the door, followed by a pause, and then two more. Before I could get to the door to open it, Leigh comes bouncing in. She takes one look at a half-naked Finn and her face is in delight as she slowly starts to back herself out of the apartment.

"Leigh, wait." I move toward her. I take a deep breath, as this will be the first time I've had to say it out loud. "I have to tell you something." Her face drops. She knows. "My brother is gone."

"Oh, no. Oh, honey." She leans in and wraps her arms around me. I'm envious of the tears that have wet her cheeks at this point. She loosens her grip and stands back. Then she gives me the same suspicious look-over Finn did earlier. Her vision cuts to Finn who then shrugs.

"You two do realize that I'm here, right?"

They both ignore my question, and Leigh turns back to me. "I'm going to leave you to your company, but if you're alone later, you call me and I'll come over."

"Thanks, Leigh. I'll let you know."

Leigh clutches me once more before walking out of the apartment. My attention returns to the man standing in my living room. The one who was just unknowingly pulled into this madness.

"You can go. Really. I'm not going to be good company. Besides, I know you're a busy guy and—"

"Not today, I'm not. I got the day off, remember?"

I nod. "I think I'm going to go for a walk."

Before I reach the bedroom to change into a pair of yoga pants that have never seen a single yoga move, Finn steps in front of me.

"If you really want me to leave, I'll leave." His voice is low and gentle. "But I would prefer not to leave you alone today."

It feels like there's something rising within me. I can feel the burn from the water trying to release from my eyes.

"I don't want you to go."

With a nod, Finn walks to the bedroom and comes back out with the shirt he was wearing yesterday.

"Let's go for a walk," he says.

I change quickly then we head out of the apartment together.

As soon as our feet hit the concrete, Finn walks in front of me. His head turns in my direction then he signals me to follow him.

"Are we walking somewhere in particular?" I ask after walking for few minutes.

"Yep. Here."

Looking around at the buildings, I don't understand.

"Where is… here?"

Finn points to the ground at a circle in the bricks.

"The Freedom Trail. It's long as hell. Two and a half miles one way to be exact. Ready?"

I shrug. Maybe I'll find some freedom by the time we're done walking this trail, but deep down I know better.

Most locals know this as a tourist attraction. It passes by some of the most historic spots in Boston. It's lined with museums, churches, and parks. Just as suspected, we pass mostly tourists on the trail. I watch their happy faces. Their body language. Each one so full of life.

"Fuck, woman," Finn says out of breath. His hand presses into his side as he puffs. My damp shirt sticks to my body. "I said walk. I didn't agree to running. I fuckin' hate running."

"I didn't even realize I was running," I pant, out of breath.

"Maybe we should take a cab back," he says.

The last thing I want to do right now is get into a stuffy cab.

"I promise I'll walk."

He nods and we begin the trek back. About halfway back to my building, a foreign feeling comes from my hand. Finn's fingers are laced within mine.

"You were pickin' up the pace, and I don't have it in me to run again. I'm a lifter, not a runner. I'll be holdin' onto you."

My hand hasn't been occupied by another in years. I had one serious boyfriend a few years back, but he just couldn't understand why I always ran to my brother. He just wanted more of my time, and I couldn't give that to him.

I stop to take a deep breath as we reach the front of my building. Having Finn around has always been something I've wanted. But right now I have problems and I refuse to make my problems, his problems. He's already called off work because of me. As long as I've worked at O'Reilly's, I can't recall a time that Finn he's ever done that.

"Thank you for walking with me. I think I'm just going to go shower off and try to get some sleep." I say.

"You think you're gonna be able to sleep?"

Everything Finn says to me, screams concern. I don't want him to analyze every move I make.

"I really want to try."

Finn moves to me, pulls me close, and wraps me up in a tight hug.

"You need me, call," he says.

"Okay."

He releases me and places his finger under my chin to lift my eyes to his. "I'm serious. You need me. Call me."

I flash him a knowing smile. He eyes me over, flashes me his dimpled grin, and walks away.

Herman comes running as soon as I open the door to my apartment. I scoop up my four-legged man and snuggle him as I walk into the bedroom. He purrs loudly when I set him on the comforter while I grab some clean clothes and head into the bathroom.

This building takes forever to get warm water so I turn on the shower and let it run as I wash my face. My blond hair cascades out of the messy bun on top of my head as I remove the elastic. The sadness in my light blue eyes stuns me as I look at myself in the mirror. The longer I look at myself, the more nauseous I become. The sickness swirls around in my stomach as my breathing increases. That clammy hot feeling runs up my arms and into my head. I know what this is. This has happened to me before. Panic.

This isn't happening. My entire life and everything I've ever known is now only memories. Lost. Broken. I don't know what to do. With the walls closing in, I jump in the shower, clothes and all. The pain in my chest rises to an unbearable level of suffocation, and my legs give out from under me. My body crumples to the floor of the shower, and finally, I let myself cry. I cry for my brother. I cry for my parents. I cry for what used to be me. I cry for the agonizing reality that I'll have to live the rest of my life knowing that I should have stayed with him. Moving here was the biggest mistake of my life and one that I'll pay for forever.

As numbness takes over my body, the tears stop flowing. I no longer feel the heat from the water pelting my skin. Time has frozen, and as long as I'm in this shower, the world outside doesn't exist. The ticking of the clock on the wall fades, and the light disappears as my eyes slowly close, losing all feeling both inside and out.

Through the darkness, I hear a bang and then muffled voices. They get louder, but my body stays still, unable to move even if I wanted to.

"Daphne?" I hear my name and more banging, though it seems far away. Suddenly, the curtain to the shower flings open, and I see a blurry outline of a person.

"Fuck. Fuck, I knew I shouldn't have left you."

I'm lifted out of the tub. Even though I'm looking at the side of Finn's face, it's still unclear what's happening. His scruffy jaw is tense and rigid. *Is he angry with me?*

"Damn it. What the hell are you tryin' to do?"

He sets me down on my bed, and it's only then I realize my body is shaking violently.

"Wh...wha...what...ha...happened?" I asked him, my teeth chattering.

The last thing I remember is looking into the mirror in the bathroom. I focus on my wet pants, trying to figure out why I didn't take my clothes off before I got into the shower as Finn runs through the apartment. Weight begins to pile on my shoulders as he places something on me and then stands back. Finn begins to rapidly pace in front of me. His hands roughly run up his face and over his head before he lets out a long, ragged breath.

"You tell me. I was gone for about an hour before I realized that I forgot my wallet on your nightstand, and when I came back, you wouldn't answer your door. Your neighbor heard me knockin' and I told her I just needed my wallet. She came in to get it and then started hollerin' for help. I came runnin' in to see you curled up in a ball in your tub, shaking and damn near blue. That water was ice cold."

Not satisfied with my current coverings, Finn places every blanket he can find in the apartment on me. The bed dips beside me and his rubs his hands up and down my arms quickly to help heat me up. A sniffle from the opposite corner of my bedroom calls my attention. Leigh leans against the windowsill, chewing her fingernails.

"Stop biting your damn nails," I say. "I'm fine. I just lost it." Apparently, I'm not done losing it. As the words leave my mouth, tears rapidly begin to fall again. They don't stop as Leigh makes some hot tea, and they don't stop as Leigh and Finn have a conversation I can't hear in the corner of the room. It's obvious neither of them know what to say to me. What can be said? They spend the rest of the day tip-toeing around me.

The light outside begins to fade before Leigh goes back to her apartment. Finn sits next to me, holding my curled up body in his large arms. Tears fall through every show we watch. After a long emotional day, Finn ordering food that I couldn't stomach to eat, and watching almost every episode of 50's comedies, I'm carried to bed. There isn't even once slice of me that has enough energy to argue with it. Finn climbs in right next to me and relief takes over.

It doesn't take long until Finn's breath steadies. Listening to the inhales and exhales soothes my nerves. However, I still can't close my eyes. All I keep hearing is my brother's last word. I hope I never hear that word again. *Sorry.* That one word was the end of his life, and it feels like the beginning of my hell.

CHAPTER THREE

MY PHONE RINGS twice before blindly reaching for it on my nightstand. "Hey, Brother." The words fall from my mouth as they had so many times before. My eyelids blink rapidly, trying to adjust to the light. The numbers on the clock finally come into focus. Nine o'clock. It feels like my heart stops beating as I wait for a response from the other end of the line.

"Hey. I wanted to make sure you're doing all right," Ryan says in a quiet voice.

I'm not sure if I blame Ryan, myself, or both of us. He was the one who was supposed to be with Jarrod, but then again, he's a grown ass man with his own life and a relationship. It's an impossible task for him to be with Jarrod every minute of every day and unrealistic for me to expect that.

"I'm doing okay."

The bed dips beside me as Finn rolls closer to watch me talk.

"Can we meet up? I mean in a few days. After Jarrod's—"

"Don't even fucking say it, Ryan. I'm not going to my mother's fiasco of a funeral. I don't want to know about it. Not one detail. I have to go." I hang up on Ryan before he can say anything about the funeral or ask me how I'm doing again. I've never understood why people ask that question after you lose someone you love. How would anyone be doing? *Not fucking great.* Is that what people actually want to hear?

"How long have you known, Ryan?" Finn asks, his voice gruff from the morning.

"Damn near all my life. I guess you could say he's like a brother, but it's not the same."

"I get that."

Stretching back out onto the bed, I stare at the ceiling.

"We're not workin' today," Finn says as he reaches for his phone on the nightstand. I reach for him and place my hand on his chest to stop him.

"I need to go to work. I have to distract myself. Just sitting around here is going to drive me nuts. If you don't want to go into work, that's your business. But I have to do something."

I don't realize that my fingers are tracing the large scar on Finn's chest until he lowers his head and stares at my hand. I get a feeling that Finn isn't comfortable with me touching it so I pull my hand back and place it on my side.

He sits up and moves out of the bed, retrieving his shirt from the top of the dresser. "It's too soon for you to be workin', don't you think?"

"Everyone handles things differently. I have to keep going, or I'm afraid I might drown."

"Fair enough. But if you go, I'm going, too. We've got a few hours. Are you going to be okay if I go home and get cleaned up, or are you gonna try hypothermia again?"

"I'll be fine." He squints his eyes at me. "Go. I'll see you at work later."

The little hairs on my arms tingle as he walks closer to me. I take a deep breath in as he leans in, places his hands on either side of me, and looks me in the eye.

"Promise me, Daffodil."

My heart picks up an extra beat.

"Daffodil?" I ask.

"New name for you."

"Why Daffodil?"

"Daffodils symbolize new beginnings. Seems like you could use one of those."

The only other person Finn has a nickname for is Sophie. I know that she's incredibly important to him because his eyes sparkle when he says her name. They sparkled in a similar same way when my new nickname came out of his mouth.

"How do you know what daffodils symbolize? I can't see you out watering the flowers."

"In Ireland, my mother's entire backyard is nothing but a garden. She loves flowers, knows everything about them and what they symbolize. She's always talkin' my ear off about it. You're definitely Daffodil," he declares.

He kisses my cheek then walks out of the apartment. Finn's tender affection is surprising, and I'm scared for what he thinks might be happening. My heart wants Finn desperately. But there's no way anything can happen between us. The guilt I feel for even just breathing is overwhelming. How can I be happy?

* * *

It's been a week since my brother's death. Each night, I work with Finn hovering over me, watching my every move. Working at the pub makes it easy to stay busy and forget about my problems. Even though working was always helpful for me to focus on something else, even while I was here, Jarrod was always on my mind. But now, with nothing else to worry about, I focus on the regulars. They're the customers who come in, take a seat at the bar, and order drink after drink. Their hands gripping onto the cool glass, desperately pouring the numbing liquor into their mouths. Finn's friend Paul is one of them. He's been coming in here once a week since Benson and Sophie's wedding. Every Wednesday night, Paul bellies up to the bar. Most of the regulars still have little glimpses of light in the backs of their eyes. That light is a sign that deep down, their soul still thrives. Paul isn't one of those regulars. His eyes are completely muted. Some would say they're black. He may flash a smile in my direction from time to time, but those are just the muscles moving.

After Sophie began dating Benson, he started coming into the bar. Finn and Benson became fast friends. Paul is Benson's driver and also his right-hand man at Knoxx Developments. The three men are now extremely close. That's the only reason he lets Paul continue to come in here. Finn doesn't put up with too much shit in the pub. But Paul has been known to start some shit around here. Anyone else would have been banned from stepping foot back into this building. I'm not sure what is eating Paul alive, but from the looks of it, it doesn't have far to go until it's completely consumed him.

I manage through my shifts, trying to make those who are sad a little happier as if I'm a happy person myself. It's easy to do at work, when I'm focusing on everyone else. But each night, my life comes crashing back down on me as I walk into my apartment and settle into the stillness. Each day does get a little better.

O'Reilly's is busy. I spot Tasha looking frazzled as always with a tray full of beers in her hands coming around the bar. She flashes me a bright white smile, then her face returns to focus on not spilling the drinks all over the place. I can't help but smile widely back at her. Tasha is one of the sweetest people I've ever met. But, we've all learned to stay a few feet away from her as she walks with a full tray though. She's clumsy as can be. Her long black hair flows behind her as she quickly walks through the pub. She's curvy in all the right places, and her mesmerizing green eyes have most of the customers drooling over her.

"Well, there's something I like to see," Kael says as he walks up to my side at the bar. "You've got tables six through ten tonight," he pauses. "Daffodil."

My lips purse together and my eyelids squeeze shut.

"What did you just call me?"

Kael eyes me disapprovingly and walks away. Damn it. Finn has been talking to Kael about me. I haven't seen Finn yet, but when I do, it's time we talk.

A few intoxicated men have been hitting on me for the last hour.

Most of the time I don't care. They don't mean any harm and, usually they tip well. However, one guy is starting to get a little touchy. I find Kael to warn him about the man who can't keep his hands to himself, which is protocol now. Instead of Kael moving to the front of the pub to watch him like he usually does, he nods and then disappears into the back. When Sophie was attacked and they were worried about her attacker possibly showing up here, they installed security cameras that could be viewed from the offices. I assume that's where he went when he doesn't return.

I deliver some drinks to one of my tables and head to check on another. The man's arm reaches out and catches me around the waist as I try to pass his table. He pulls me into him and I fall in his lap. Before I can even try to right myself, I feel a gentle but firm hand grip my arm. My body flies off of the man's lap and I'm lifted into the air. I get passed from one set of arms to Kael's. He sets me back on my feet away from the commotion. Finn yanks the guy out of his stool, and the repeated sound of the man getting socked in the stomach makes me jump. Kael grabs Finn's shoulder to stop him, then they both escort the drunk out of the pub. I stand, flabbergasted at Finn's response. He's been known to be a bit hot-headed and throw a few fists around. But this wasn't his normal kidney shots. He seemed enraged.

When they both walk back in, I'm still where Kael set me down.

"Daffodil," Finn says, a little winded. "You okay?"

His fucking dimple taunts me as he flashes a slight smirk and continues walking right past me. My eyes follow him into the back office. Then I stomp back there myself.

"What are you doing, Finn?" I ask him, stepping into the office.

"Protecting what's mine."

"I'm not yours. We need to talk." I take a deep breath and brace myself. The last thing I want to do is hurt him. He leans back in his office chair and crosses his arms across his chest. "You have been nothing but kind to me. I value our friendship and this job. But I think we should keep it as friends. The sex should not have happened; it gave you the wrong idea. That's my fault. I don't deserve you."

A smile appears across Finn's face, and I zone in on the small, concave comma that appears next to his mouth. He slowly gets up from his chair and walks so close to me that my breath hitches before he passes by. Finn shuts the door and the click of the lock invades my ears. I beg my body not to respond, but it doesn't listen to my head when it comes to Finn. The excitement begins to build inside of me, even though I'm fighting it.

"Finn. I'm not sure you're getting it."

"Oh, I get it. I'm not sure you do." His hand gently touches the side of my face, and he places a soft kiss on my lips, which uncontrollably kiss him back.

"That's just going to make this worse. Why are you doing this?" I whisper to him, as my head presses against his cheek.

"For so long, I've seen nothing but cheap women and the dark walls of this pub. Now all I see are fuckin' daffodils."

The warmth leaves my lips and he walks back to his chair behind the desk. An unusual move for him, especially after he locked the door.

"I don't think getting into a relationship is a good idea," I say. "I can't promise I'm going to be worth it right now."

"I'm not talking about getting into one; we're already in it. I don't let too many people into my world. I know what you're tryin' to say. You're tellin' me you don't feel what I feel. But the way your body stops when I come into sight, the way your fingertips dig into my back, the way your eyes gleam with desire when you look at me, all say otherwise. I stopped myself so many times when my hands just wanted to feel your soft skin. That's over."

"Why? If that's how you felt for so long, then why not just come out and say it? I thought what we did was just a fling for you. I never picked up on anything else."

"I thought you had a man. Thought you would leave here and go to him. It wasn't my business why you would come to me. I'm not the type of guy who helps someone cheat. But, I couldn't help how I felt. So I was greedy and took whatever you would give me. The minute I found out the truth, was the minute you became mine."

I slowly walk around the desk. Reaching Finn's side, he angles his head to look at my face. His hand gently moves up my thigh and rests on my hip. A moment of weakness takes over and things begin to fall from my mouth that I never intended to say to Finnegan O'Reilly.

"I've wanted you for so long. I just couldn't put someone in front of Jarrod. You deserve better than that. Someone who would put you first. And now with Jarrod gone, there's just so much to process right now."

"While you process, I'm here." He rises from the chair and caresses my cheek with his bleeding hand. "For the record. You will always be worth it."

Finn takes his seat behind his desk again and begins typing away on his keyboard. I'm sure the redness from his sweet words has risen into my cheeks so I make my way back to the office door.

"Finn?"

"Yeah?"

"Your hand is bleeding."

"Aw damn it! There goes my manicure this week."

I laugh all the way down the hall as I return to my tables to cash them out for the night.

I'm so glad it's time to go home. I need a little time to myself.

"Hey," Kael greets me as finishing up my closing duties.

"Hey yourself," I say back.

"What's really going on between you and my brother?"

"You are just as subtle as they come, aren't you?" I snicker, trying to brush off his question.

"I'm serious, Daphne. What's going on?"

"Nothing…Well, I don't really know."

He takes in a louder than normal breath. "You have a lot going on right now. I think you should focus on getting yourself straight. Finn can be tough to crack, but once you're in, he falls fast and deep. The last time his heart was broken, he was devastated. We almost lost this bar. I won't sit by and watch that happen again."

Finn doesn't strike me as a guy who gets his feelings hurt so easily. This girl must have done something terrible to him. I feel the warmth of adrenaline gathering in the pit of my stomach as anger washes over me. I'm surprised by my own reaction to someone hurting Finn. How do I even respond to Kael? I don't even know what the fuck I'm doing. But I know how I feel about Finn. There's just no way I can make that kind of promise. All I seem to be able to do is nod my head even though it isn't an agreement.

"Shit," Kael mumbles under his breath. "I don't like this." His voice trails off the further he gets from me as he walks away.

I finish up quickly, race to the front door, and yell to the back, "I'm out." Once I'm outside of the pub, I take off running to get around the corner as fast as I can before one of the O'Reilly brothers confronts me again. Not two steps after my pace slows, my phone rings.

I don't even look. I know who it is.

"Look I--"

"You avoidin' me now?"

"No. Well, kind of. I just need a little bit of time to get my thoughts straight. I won't be good for anyone until I straighten this jagged ass line that I've been walking since I was a kid. I want to be good for you, Finn. I need to figure out how."

"Do what you need to do. I don't give a fuck if it's five in the morning. You need me, call."

"I will."

I love walking home at night. The air seems a little lighter. The world a little quieter. It calms me. Until I spot a man leaned against the railing halfway up the stairs of my building. Adrenaline kicks in as I get closer. My muscles relax as his familiar facial features become clear. Ryan's angled jaw opens as a small snore comes out of his mouth. I can't believe he's sitting on the dirty cement in his stupid designer pants. He looks like everyone else in the group my parents associate with. That's how he and my brother met and became so close. Our parents have been friends since we were babies.

He wasn't like them though. He was kind and compassionate and didn't care what anyone thought of him. Though he still dressed like an idiot. Confused as to why he was now sitting on my stoop at this hour of the morning, and looking incredibly out of place, I kick his stupid seven-hundred-dollar loafer. He startles and stands up, disoriented, and nearly falls down the stairs.

"Shit, you scared the hell out of me."

"What are you doing here?" I ask him, annoyed. I was looking forward to eating a pint of ice cream all by myself and scarfing down the leftover pizza in my fridge when I got home.

"I don't believe that you're as okay as you say you are. I took some time off of work to come stay with you for a few days."

I look to the sky in defeat. Running away sounds really great after the last few days I've had. A nice sunny tropical island is calling my name. Ryan is the last person on this planet that I want to see right now.

"Ever think I just want to be alone?"

His face drops, signaling that I've hurt his feelings.

"For crying out loud, c'mon," I say, walking past him to the door.

I let us into the building and up to my apartment. Ryan has never been here because I was always going to Albany. Part of me is wondering how he even knows where I live, but Jarrod probably had my address somewhere around the house.

Opening my door, my favorite man greets me, and I plop down on the floor for our ritual. Ryan just gives me a weird look as he steps around me.

"Wow, this is a nice place. Small but nice."

"Is that a compliment or a jab?"

"It was a compliment. Calm down."

"I'm just tired." I flash Ryan a halfhearted smiled and get a knowing nod in return.

"This place fits you, I can see why you like it here so much. It's like a different world from where we grew up."

"That's exactly what I was looking for when I found it. Look, I'm going to bed. You can crash on the couch. I'll grab you some blankets and a pillow."

"Cool. We'll talk tomorrow about what we're going to do."

"What do you mean, what we're going to do?"

"Well, I'm here. I want to see Boston. Figured you could show me around."

"And how do you know I don't have to work tomorrow?"

"Jarrod has your schedule on the fridge."

Sadness takes over both of our faces. "I don't know if I'm up to it. I'll think about it tomorrow. I'm exhausted."

After I get Ryan all set up on my couch for the night, I shut my bedroom door and lay in bed thinking about my brother. He loved Ryan like a brother, even though Ryan can be a bit irritating sometimes. Like showing up unannounced. But then I start to think about Finn and what he said today. Maybe I'll just play this out day by day and see where it leads us.

I toss and turn for most of the early morning hours. I fall asleep for short intervals, waking up then falling back asleep again. Within the last twenty minutes I've watched the room lighten as the sun rises outside. The bed feels too good to get out of and I don't want to deal with the world yet. I hear a faint knock then the front door open. Finn's voice comes booming through the apartment, and I fly out of bed, racing to my bedroom door. The handle makes a loud sound as I fling the door open to see Ryan standing at the front door in his boxers. Running out of my apartment, I watch Finn's back as he hustles down the stairs. I glance back at Ryan and I know what this looks like. Panic rises as my eyes are drawn to down to my feet. Beautiful, bright yellow daffodils, all over the ground.

CHAPTER FOUR

"WHAT DO you think you're doing?" The harsh tone of my voice echoes through the apartment building.

"I didn't do anything!"

"What the hell did you say to him?"

"I told him my name. That's all I got in before he threw the flowers down and stormed off."

The pounding in my chest grows more intense as the seconds pass.

"Put some fucking clothes on," I demand before bolting down the stairs after Finn.

The bottoms of my naked feet begin to hurt as I jog across the sidewalk and to the edge of the street. Looking in both directions, Finn isn't anywhere in sight. I nearly jump out of my skin when a horn blares from the side road next to my building. My head tilts to the sky and I blow out a large puff of air. The driver's side window is down and Finn nods at me. Trying hard not to step on any rocks, I gingerly walk up to the black Wrangler.

"Finn, nothing happened between us." Even the thought makes me want to vomit. I scrunch my nose in disgust. "Nor will it ever."

"I didn't think you did."

"If you didn't think that, then why did you throw those flowers all over the ground and take off?"

"If I didn't leave, I was gonna knock his ass out. I know he's your friend. But seein' another dude in your apartment in his boxers, didn't sit well with me. I needed to go and fast. Was just gettin' ready to call you."

My shoulders release the tension they were filled with. Finn steps out of the Jeep, comes in close, and puts his hands on my hips. He leans in and his lips touch mine. The kiss was innocent in the beginning. But it quickly becomes fevered. His hand travels from my hip to the nape of my neck. Pulling me further into him. His fingertips press harder into my skin.

"Fuck, Daffodil. We're in the middle of the damn street and I could take you right here. I should step back."

He isn't the only one feeling the fire burning inside. I smile seductively "Why? You against having sex in a car?" I'm only half joking as I nod toward the Wrangler with a grin on my face.

"I'm done having you in places where I can't make you scream my name. The next time I'm inside you, you're goin' to find out just how much I've been holding back. There ain't enough room in the Wrangler for that."

"Oh," I say, not having any other response to that.

"When is your houseguest leaving? Soon, I hope."

"I'm not sure. I had no idea he even knew where I lived. When I came home last night, he was passed out on my stoop. He wants me to show him around Boston tonight."

Finn reaches into his pocket while making a ringing sound with his mouth. He pretends to hit a button on his cell phone, then puts it up to his ear. "Hey, Kael. What's that? You need Daphne to work tonight? Okay, I'll tell her." He pretends to hang up the phone and looks at me with a shitty grin on his face. "Kael says we need you to come into work tonight."

"You're ridiculous," I say to him, laughing. "Ryan must be having a rough time about my brother. Jarrod would have wanted me to be here for him. I'll take him out tonight and hopefully, he'll decide to go home tomorrow."

"There's somethin' about him that rubs me the wrong way. I don't know what it is. But, I don't like it."

"He's a huge pain in the ass, but he's harmless. He just has an ego the size of a country."

Finn gives me a cautious eye, and I can tell he's trying to figure out what to say.

"Text me and let me know where you're at later. I'm going home to crash for a few hours before work."

He pulls me into a deep kiss before releasing me and hopping into his Wrangler. I head back up to my apartment to have a little chat with Ryan.

As I march through my door, Ryan is already dressed, has folded the blankets, and placed the pillow neatly on top. He's standing in the kitchen and looking at me dumbfounded while sipping a cup of coffee.

"Do not come into my home and answer the door in your underwear. Why the fuck were you in your boxers?"

"It's how I sleep. I had just gotten up and was heading to the bathroom when he came to the door. You were sleeping and I didn't want the knocking to wake you up, so I answered it. Thought I was doing you a favor. It was just a misunderstanding, Daphs."

"Ugh. Don't call me that and don't do that shit again. If you sleep here, you wear pants. Jesus. I'm going to take a shower and get cleaned up, and then we'll go get something to eat. I'll show you around, and we'll go out to a few bars later. I have to work tomorrow, so—"

"That sounds cool. Can't wait to check out Boston," he says, excited, as if I'm not flaming pissed at him.

* * *

MOST OF THE morning is spent visiting a few of the classic tourist stops in Boston then we hit a chowder hut for lunch. All of our conversations seem to turn to memories of Jarrod. Most of them make us break out in laughter. But a few of the more precious memories bring a mist to both of our eyes. The day reminds me that even though Ryan drives me absolutely nuts, he's just as much a part of my family as Jarrod was. He may be the only one that truly knows exactly what I went through. Sometimes, I forget that he went through the same thing.

* * *

"ARE YOU ALMOST READY? GOOD GRIEF," I shout through the bathroom door to Ryan. He takes longer to get ready than four high school girls getting ready for prom.

I glance in the full length mirror on the wall to double check my clothes. My favorite pair of black skinny jeans are tucked partially into my high-heeled, peek-a-boo toe boots. I brush a few cat hairs off of my army green, loose-fitting, V-neck shirt. My hair is teased into a bouffant in the front, pulled slick on the sides, then into a ponytail in the back. It's my usual going-out hairdo. Unlike Ryan, it takes me about ten minutes.

As I wait an eternity for Ryan to get ready, I text Finn and let him know we'll be at Zuco's first. Before I get my phone tucked back into my pocket, it chimes with a return text from Finn.

BE CAREFUL, keep me updated. If you need me, call.

AN UNCONTROLLABLE SMILE spreads across my face. One quick glance in the mirror shows the rosy color that has taken over my cheeks. *Get it under control, Daphne.* I don't know what's going to happen with Finn, but I'm really fucking excited to find out. Every time Finn touches me, the sparks ignite the fire that I've held deep within me for years. I'm scared, but at the same time, I'm so sick of holding back.

Ryan finally steps out of the bathroom. The two of us could not be more opposite. His khaki Dockers are freshly pressed with a sharp crease down the center of each pant leg. A white button-down collared shirt is tucked into the pants and rolled halfway up his forearms. His hair looks like a purposeful mess, but he keeps tussling with it in the mirror.

"Are you about done? Christ, you fuss more than any girl I've ever known." Without waiting for his answer, I grab my black cross-body purse and sling it over my shoulder.

"Yeah, yeah, let's go," he says, still messing with his hair. It still looks a damn mess.

Just as I step out of the door, I jump at the sound of Leigh's voice.

"Hey, girl! You finally ready?"

"Ready for what?" I ask her, confused. *Shit. Did I schedule something with her and forget?* That happens often unfortunately, as I'm an unorganized disaster most of the time.

"I'm going out with you guys tonight. Finn said you wanted me to go."

"Oh he did, did he?" Another smile comes over my face. I know what he's doing. He isn't a fan of Ryan. But apparently, he is a fan of Leigh's. By sending her with me, he has an extra set of eyes on me. Tricky bastard. He's lucky I love Leigh so much and I'm glad she's coming, or I'd be really pissed that he overstepped.

"Girl, you've got it bad," she whispers to me. Then her attention turns to Ryan. "Hey, you must be Ryan." She reaches her hand out to shake his.

"I am, and you are?" He flashes his expensive veneers in her direction and he's using his flirty voice.

"She is married with a toddler, and you have a girlfriend," I blurt out.

"Wow. Okay, ignore her rudeness. I'm Leigh, her neighbor, and whether she likes it or not, her best friend." She throws a snarky smile in my direction.

Leigh and I have no idea what it is about each other that drew us together. She's pretty much the exact opposite of me. Her world would consist of baby pink everything. She likes her appearance to be neat and crisp, opposed to my casual "just grabbed this shirt out of the dryer" style. I'm obsessed with tattoos and love the black and gray mandala ink that cascades from my shoulder to my wrist on my right arm. She would die before a needle with ink ever touched her perfect porcelain skin. Shit, the more I think about it, she's like Ryan in a lot of ways. The thing I love most about her though, is her ability to be herself around me. When she comes over on my nights off and her husband is home with Landon, she comes in her pajamas and will plop herself down on my couch. She's a great listener and is always honest with me, even when I don't want to hear the truth. She's helped me survive through a lot of Jarrod's issues, which I turned into my own. Most of all, she's never judged me. I'll love her for that forever.

"Looks like our party of two just turned into a party of three. Let's roll," I say, and head down the stairs. I'm somewhat relieved and excited that Leigh is getting a night out, too. Maybe tonight will be more fun than I thought it was going to be.

We walk into an extremely busy Zucos and immediately make our way to the bar. Before we can get our order to the bartender, Ryan's phone starts blowing up. Again. It was going off all day long. Sometimes he would excuse himself to go answer it, but most of the time, he just kept ignoring the calls. This time, he answers it.

"Ally, I told you. I'm out. I'll call you tomorrow," he huffs then hangs up.

Something suddenly doesn't seem right.

"Who was that?" I ask tentatively.

Ryan shrugs, but I know Ally must be his girlfriend—and he just blew her off. Maybe he's having a harder time with my brother's death than he's leading on.

"Why didn't Ally come with you?" I ask. "She could have come, too. I mean, you're already here. What's another person?"

He doesn't answer my question as the bartender comes to us for our order.

"I'll have a Jack and Coke," Ryan says.

"Sweet Poison," I announce.

"Hi, there. I'll have a dirty martini please, ma'am." The bartender gives an amused look to Leigh and then nods to get our drinks.

"Jesus, Leigh. This is a bar. You don't have to be all proper; she just needs your order quick so she can get to the next line of people over there." I point to the mass of people that have formed at the other end of the bar. Leigh just rolls her eyes at me.

The bartender delivers our drinks and Ryan pays for all of them. I laugh again as the bartender slides Leigh's drink to her, and Leigh replies, "Thank you so much."

"What the fuck is that?" Ryan asks, pointing to my drink.

"It's a Sweet Poison. Two types of rum and curacao with pineapple juice."

Ryan's face twists, but I couldn't give a shit less. Every once in a while, I'll go for rum instead of my usual Jameson. I'll get buzzed, but it rarely gets me drunk and I never get a hangover from it. That's the trick with liquor. If you know how certain liquors affect you, you can avoid the shitty feeling the next day.

After a round of pool, we decided to stay at Zucos instead of hitting more bars. I text Finn to let him know that we'll be here for the rest of the night then shove my phone into my back pocket.

"I can't believe you hustled me," I say to Leigh.

"I didn't hustle you. You never asked if I had ever played pool before. Completely not my fault."

Leigh has beat us all three games of pool. How was I supposed to know that her father had a pool table in their basement growing up?

Ryan brings another round of drinks to the pool table. Leigh seems to be having the time of her life. Hell, she's a one-woman show as she dances to the music. She doesn't get out much and it makes me happy to see her having so much fun.

"Come to the bathroom with me," Leigh says, and she grabs my hand to drag me along with her. I've never understood women going to the bathroom together, but I go anyways.

"We'll be right back," I say to Ryan, and he nods because he's gotten himself into some conversation about baseball with a guy next to us.

"I tell you, if I never met Carter and I didn't love him dearly, I'd be all over Ryan," Leigh says through the bathroom stall.

"I'm seriously going to pretend you didn't just say that right now.

Remind me to thank Carter that he found you and married you before Ryan came anywhere near you."

Leigh's laugh echoes in the bathroom as she exits the stall and washes her hands while singing the Happy Birthday song. She sings it every time she washes her hands because someone told her that song is exactly how long it takes to get all the germs off. I just shake my head and fan myself. It's hot in here.

Leigh reaches into her pale pink purse and reapplies her nude lip color before we exit the bathroom. As we approach our table, Ryan is still talking to his newly found buddy. Done with getting my ass kicked at pool, I nod for Leigh to come and sit with me at the high table that lines the wall next to the pool table we were playing at. Ryan sees us and puts up one finger, indicating he'll be there in one second and then points to two new drinks he must have ordered us while we were in the bathroom. The crowd has thinned out, and it isn't as busy as it was when we first arrived.

Ryan finally stops talking and grabs a pool stick to break.

"I don't want to play anymore," I whine.

"I'm in," Leigh shouts and jumps down from her chair.

"Dammit." I give in and jump off my stool too and prepare to get whooped. After a couple of turns, I can't get over the fact that I feel so hot.

"Is it hot in here to you guys?"

"No, I'm fine," Leigh says, giving me a slight side eye.

"I'm good," Ryan says as he takes his turn and misses his shot.

"I'm going to the bathroom and splash some water on my face real quick. I'll be right back."

"Want me to go with you?" Leigh asks, looking a bit concerned.

"No, I don't need a chaperone to pee," I snip, jokingly with her.

Halfway to the bathroom, the sick feeling intensifies. It feels like the room gained a hundred degrees in the last three seconds. The bathroom door slams against the wall as I throw it open. I can't get to the sink fast enough and begin splashing cold water on my face. It doesn't seem to be helping. The room tilts and I lean against the wall to hold myself up. Desperate to rid my head of the spinning, I close my eyes. That was a horrible idea. They shoot open and Leigh comes through the bathroom door just as my legs give out from under me. She rushes to my side and tries to haul me up to my feet, but I can't get my legs to work. Giving up, she reaches for her phone.

Leigh's voice echoes in the bathroom. "Finn, Daphne just collapsed in the—"

"I got her." Ryan's voice sounds far away though I feel his skinny arms go around my legs and back. He struggles to get me off of the floor. I close my eyes again to try to avoid the spinning. But combined with the movement of Ryan carrying me, it only makes it worse. Cool air hits my skin and exhaustion hits me.

My vision is turning fuzzy when suddenly I hear a booming voice. "Get. Your. Fucking. Hands. Off. Her."

"It's cool. Chill out. She's like a sister to me. I've known her my entire life. I'll take care of her."

"I don't care. Give her to me or I swear to God, I'll fucking break you into pieces."

The jostle makes my stomach turn but the world is growing darker as the fatigue takes over. His large and familiar arms hold me so closely against him. A whisper invades my ear as I clutch his shirt.

"I've got you, Daffodil."

CHAPTER FIVE

THE THROBBING in my head is something I haven't felt since my twenty-first birthday. *What happened?* Finn's voice is the last thing I remember. Even the pale light from the window burns my eyes. Herman meows at the end of my bed and I know I'm home. Getting hit by a Mac truck probably feels better than how I'm feeling right now. The black Stones t-shirt flows loosely over my skin. *Oh, fuck no.* Who the hell changed my clothes?

Just as I'm about to try to get out of bed, Finn comes walking through my bedroom door. His eyes meet mine and narrow. I've only seen Finn get mad at work. Like when the drunks get out of line and start getting aggressive with the staff. His facial expressions alone can be downright scary. And he doesn't look too happy right about now.

"Hey," he says curtly.

"What happened?" I press my eyelids together tightly mostly because my head is killing me. But also because I'm not even sure I want to know the answer to that.

"I don't know, but I don't fuckin' like it."

"Where's Ryan?"

"Where he should be."

A million thoughts run through my mind. *What did Finn do to Ryan?*

"And where exactly is that?"

"He went back to Albany. I told him to get the fuck out this mornin'. Hope that doesn't piss you off, but right now, I don't care."

Finn hands me a couple of aspirin and a glass of water. The pills scratch my throat as they go down but I chug that water as if I had just spent ten days on the Sahara.

The pillows cushion my body as I sink back down. I guess I won't be getting up after all. Without words, Finn grabs the empty glass and leaves the room. A few minutes later he returns with hot tea. He places it on the table next to me, then turns to walk away.

"Come here."

Finn walks slowly back to me but he doesn't sit down. Reaching up, I put my hand to his face and cup his cheek. The anger that was in his eyes fades to concern.

"I...I don't know what happened."

My hand falls back to me as I lose his cheek. The heavy sound of his footsteps vibrate in my head as he walks around the bed. I brace for the heavy thud of his shoes as he kicks them off to climb in next to me. He stretches out on his back and tucks both hands under his head.

"Leigh called me—"

"Oh my God! Leigh."

I bolt up in a panic but Finn catches me by the shoulder, and pulls me back down.

"She's fine and at home. Don't worry. You, on the other hand, were some kind of fucked up. I had a bad feeling in my gut all day. I finally gave in and was on my way to join you before Leigh called. When I pulled up and his fuckin' hands were holding you, I saw flat-out red. Because he means somethin' to you, I let him live. Since he was drinkin' he had to stay here last night. But there was no way in hell I was leavin' you alone with him here."

"Are you jealous? Of a man who is like a brother to me no less."

"Jealous? No. Instinct? Absolutely."

Finn has never shown jealous tendencies. With anyone else, at any other time, I would have a huge problem with this. But I know Finn is just being overprotective of me right now.

"I've never had that type of reaction to rum," I say, still so confused.

"You've been going through a lot. Maybe you weren't payin' attention to how many you had. The only thing I do know right now is that you were out cold, in the middle of the night, at a bar. None of that sits well with me."

All of this drama is too much for me to even try to stay awake. I'm so over last night and this day. Finn must see the exhaustion on my face as he lifts the covers back up to my chin and kisses my forehead before he walks to the door.

"I'll be in the living room," he whispers, then leaves the room.

AFTER A COUPLE of hours lying in bed trying to get rid of this horrid headache, I give up. The only thing I've been able to do is think, which is never good. Seeing my phone on the nightstand, I reach for it. There's no telling why I feel like making myself feel as shitty as possible today. Maybe it's because I'm longing to hear that familiar voice. It's going to be for nothing. But here I am, dialing his phone number. The phone shakes against my head as the rings comes through the speaker. One…two…three…

"Hello," the gruff voice on the other end makes my heart ache just a little.

"Hi, Daddy." My voice is small and meek as if there's a different person that takes over me when talking to my father.

"Hey there, baby. You doing okay? I've been worried about—" My father's voice gets cut off by my mother, who obviously just walked into the room.

"Who's on the phone, Harrold?" she asks. I know from living with them for so long that his long pause was a good sign he's trying to determine my mother's mood and whether he should tell her it's me on the other end.

"It's Daphne, dear. Do you want to say hello?"

"No. Tell her I love her." Her voice is curt and snippy, as if the words are obligatory. How could a mother feel that way? Deep down, I think she has love *for* me. I just don't think she likes that she does. "We have to go now. We're going to be late. Hang up now, Harrold." Her voice is far away but I can still hear her clearly through the phone.

"I have to go, baby. I'll call you when I have some time to chat, okay? Bye."

The line cuts off before I can get out my words.

"Bye, Daddy," I whisper.

I don't know why I keep trying. This happens every time he answers. One sentence is spoken before she walks in and rushes him off of the phone. Before he hangs up, he tells me he'll call and then he never does. Unlike my mother, I know he loves me. But, she keeps him on a tight leash, even with his own daughter.

Sitting back against the headboard, I think about what it might be like to have an entire conversation with him, just the two of us. I'm a far cry from what my mother tried to mold me to be. The opposite of the elite young lady she wanted. She can't brag about her daughter who lives in a tiny apartment in Boston, works at an Irish pub at night, dresses in mostly black, and has tattoos.

The door to my bedroom opens slowly as Finn cautiously enters. His eyes scan my face. "You okay?"

I forgot he was here. And since my bedroom door was still cracked, I'm sure he heard that phone call. Or lack thereof.

"I'm fine." His fingers stroke my cheek. "I take it you heard my conversation." He nods. "That's nothing new. I'm used to it." I pause, then sit up. "I'm starving, believe that shit or not. You want to go get some food before we head in to work?"

"I already ordered some. I was just coming in here to wake you up to come eat when I heard you talkin' on the phone."

Finn pulls the covers back, and my naked legs crawl out of the bed. With my headache still hanging on, I painfully walk out to the living room. Once in there, I realize that I was only followed by Herman. "Finn?" I call back through the apartment.

With his head titled down, he slowly appears from the bedroom. He leans against the door frame, crosses his arms, and proceeds to bite his bottom lip.

"What?" I ask.

"I'm havin' a real fucking hard time here, Daffodil."

I understand what Finn means until my vision drifts past his arms and I see the swell in his loose-fitted dark denim jeans. His lazy eyes drift from mine down the length of me, and I realize that I only have on my t-shirt and underwear.

"You're fuckin' gorgeous."

The atmosphere in the room changes and goosebumps appear on my forearms. His lustrous eyes penetrate down my skin. They linger in certain areas. My body tingles as if his eyes were physically touching me. Teasing me. I want him. I want every single piece of this man standing in front of me. I'm sure my head still hurts but I'm not feeling any kind of pain right now. I saunter toward him.

"Oh, Christ. Don't do that. Don't do that to me now," he says.

I turn quickly back to the kitchen but only get one before Finn spins me around and presses his needy lips against mine. Our hands wildly grab onto each other, moving rapidly across skin and through hair. The sudden loss of his heat takes me by surprise as he quickly moves back from me. His eyes move from me to the floor in front of him. "There's nothing I want more than to feel every inch of you. But I have to go open the pub and if I don't stop now, it won't open for the rest of the day."

His eyes follow my every step as I make my way to the living room and plop down on the couch. He walks to me, places his index finger under my chin, and angles my head up.

"Tonight, you're mine. Every inch of your precious skin is going to know what my lips feel like against it. I've been waiting for this. I've been waiting for you. Tonight, it's you and me." His lips press softly on mine. His warm tongue slips inside and rolls across mine. Desperate to hold on, my fingers slip into the back of his hair, and our kiss intensifies. He groans deeply as he pulls away. "You sure you're feeling up to comin' in?"

"Yep. I'll be there."

"This could be the most amount of torture I've ever been through." He swipes his hand from his forehead to his chin. You need me, call."

With his usual farewell, he leaves my apartment. Two seconds later, I get a familiar knock on my front door. Leigh opens it slightly.

"C'mon in," I say.

She lunges inside, and slams the door behind her. She looks overly excited today. I bounce as she plops down on the couch next to me.

"What is going on with you and the Hulk? It's obviously more than what you've told me, so don't even try to hide it. Spill."

A loud puff of air spills from my lungs. "I don't know, Leigh. I didn't think I was ready to be in a relationship. But, I've known Finn for years. I've *liked* him for years. And I feel like I could be really happy with him. I feel safe with him. Protected."

"Oh, I already know that. I swear, he was there in, what seemed like, a minute. Speaking of last night, I've never seen you sick like that. You scared me."

"I know. I---" I'm interrupted by the sound of paper bags. Leigh starts opening the takeout bags on my coffee table, hauling out the food that Finn ordered for me. As I reach for a fry and shove it in my mouth, I'm astounded by the amount of food sitting in front of us. Two different types of soups, a greasy cheeseburger with fries, and two street tacos. I reach for the cheeseburger as Leigh helps herself to one of the tacos.

"I have no clue what happened last night. My only guess is that I just overdid it. I wasn't keeping track of how many I had. It felt good to not think about anything for a little while, including Jarrod. Fuck, that sounds awful, doesn't it?"

"No, it doesn't. You've been taking care of him your entire life. Always worrying and thinking about where he is or what he's doing. Having to take off work for your unexpected trips back and forth to Albany. It takes a toll. You're entitled to start thinking about yourself for once and what you want out of life. It doesn't mean that you love him any less. It means it's your time now."

"I know but…"

"No." Leigh's firm voice fills the room. She puts her hand on top of mine and her kind smile returns. "It's your time now."

* * *

IN THE MIDDLE of putting on my black eyeliner, the phone chimes with a text from Finn.

We have enough coverage for tonight if you want to take off. You might need the extra rest for when I get there.

His text message sends me into a giggle fit.

I'll be in, and the only one who might need the rest is you.

With a fresh face of makeup and my favorite short romper on, I head out. The thought of what tonight will have in store is the only thing I can think about as I watch my studded sandals take step after step. The weather today is teasing of summer so I couldn't resist pulling them out, even though I'm sure we'll still be getting a couple colder days.

Halfway to work, my phone rings. I get excited but only for a second before I see who it is.

"Ryan," I answer.

"Hey, what the fuck?" he blurts into the phone.

"Excuse me? You call me and that's how you greet me?"

"Your fucking boyfriend kicked me out of your house. Who does he think he is? I've known you my whole damn life, Daphne Jones. He has no right to kick me out of your house. You better tell him to chill out."

"He was being protective. I'll talk to him, but you need to chill out, too. He's not too happy with how you answered my door yesterday. Remember?"

"Whatever. I called because you went down pretty quick. Do you remember much of anything?"

"I don't remember anything after going into Finn's arms. I guess I better start paying closer attention to how much I'm drinking. Why are you so worried about me all of the sudden? Don't you have a girlfriend you should be worried about? I mean, what the hell is going on with you two?"

"Nothing is going on. We're great." He almost sounds believable.

"I'm almost to work, so I've got to go."

"Fine. Talk to you later."

"Bye."

Walking into the bar, it's obvious why Finn gave me the option to stay home. Only a few of the regulars are sitting at the bar and all but one table in the front are empty. The little hairs on the back of my neck stand up, just like they always do when I stand at this register. The cold air blows straight down in this spot which we usually love when we're running around here like crazy. I turn from the computer and begin to walk to the customer at the bar when Tasha walks right into me.

"Oh no," she calls out, but it's too late. There's pale ale all over the front of my romper. "Oh shit! Daphne, I'm so sorry, I'm so so sorry. Shit they are gonna fire me for sure."

"First, calm down. It's not a big deal, and if I have anything to say about it, you aren't going anywhere."

Tasha's face drops and her chin quivers. I place my hands on her shoulders and look at her eye to eye.

"Don't worry. If you clean it up real quick, I'll go get you another beer."

She nods her head quickly and grabs the mop from the corner as I fill a new glass with beer from the tap.

"Thank you, Daphne. You're the best."

As soon as she turns away from me, I smile and roll my eyes. Looking to my wet romper, I'm thankful that it's one of my black ones. The. dark fabric doesn't show its wet, but it definitely feels it. Focused on holding the wet fabric away from my body, I'm not looking where I'm going on my way to the bathroom and run right into Finn's hard body. He grabs my arms and quickly pins me to the wall in the corner of the hallway. My face contorts as the cold material is now squished against me.

"I wanted you to stay home today, but you just couldn't listen, could you? I've had to watch you move that body into my bar, knowing I can't have you until later. Do you know what that's doing to a man like me?"

Heat rises up within me as his body pushes even closer. He presses his face to the side of mine, and my eyes close as his breath tickles my ear with his whispers.

"I'm going to…why are you all wet?" he exclaims as he stands back to take a look at me.

A big wide grin takes over my face."Tasha."

The loud chuckle that comes from Finn, is much louder than the noise coming from bar. "Oh no," he says still laughing. "You want to go home and change?"

"No. I'm just going to stick it under the dryer in the bathroom for a few minutes," I giggle.

The laughing stops and Finn's face narrows. "Are you about to be half naked in that bathroom?"

I just smile at Finn as I slip from out of his arms and into the bathroom.

"Fuck. Me," he says to the sky before rubbing his face and heading back into the office.

I watch him walk until the door fully shuts and I lock it.

The rest of the night, I can't help but antagonize poor Finn. At one point, I brush past him to get to the back and his hand gently moves across the lower part of my belly so I move as slow as I can without actually stopping. Each flirtatious move causes Finn to chuckle and groan in my ear. Even though I'm semi-torturing Finn, I'm torturing myself, too. Feeling his warm breath against my skin every time he gets close causes the wetness to increase below. All I can think about is Finn in my bed at the end of the night. The drink orders aren't helping me either. Sex on the Beach. Slippery Panties. Screw Up Against the Wall. All night, tortured by drinks. I've never gotten all my closing duties done so fast in the entire time I've worked at O'Reilly's. My last duty is to cash out for the night. As I'm at the computer behind the bar, I can feel his presence behind me.

"You ready, Daffodil? Kael will finish everything."

"I am," I say, turning to him with a smirk. Leaning down, my breasts gently graze him as I put my apron under the bar. Suddenly, Finn's hand encloses around mine as he pulls me around the bar and toward the door. He yells back to Kael, "We're out." Still holding my hand firmly, he turns the corner and starts walking in the direction of my apartment. My head turns around looking for his Wrangler in his usual place on the side of the pub, but it's not there.

"Where's your Wrangler?"

"I parked it on the side street by your house earlier. I had a feeling it was going to be like this by the end of the night, and if I had to try to find a parking spot, I'd probably park the fuckin' thing in the middle of the road to get you upstairs."

I never thought a man would be able to make me blush, but the heat is rushing through every inch of my body.

Reaching my building, he moves aside so that I can let us in. He grabs my hand again and leads me up the stairs to my front door. As I'm putting the key into the lock, I hear Leigh's door open and turn to see her smile like the little devil she is as she sinks back into her apartment. I smile and shake my head, because I know what she's thinking and she's right.

Finn's hand rests on the small of my back as we enter my tiny home. He moves to the side, already predicting my moves before they happen. I sink to the floor, and Herman comes running into my arms.

The front door closes and I hear the click of the lock. Finn stands against the wall staring at me as I'm on the floor like an idiot petting my cat when I have other things to be doing.

"I know that cat's important to you, but if you don't speed up your greeting, I might just spontaneously combust."

I laugh and gently push Herman from my lap. Finn lifts me from the floor, causing me to squeal. Instead of setting me down on my feet, he adjusts me against his body with ease and carries me straight to my bed.

Laying me down, the speed of his movements are slow as his hands graze from the sides of my breasts to my hips. He leans in, and his hungry lips touch mine. Right then, right in that very moment, I realize just how much I want this. How long I've wanted him and how much time we've wasted. I want everything. His mind, his body, and his heart. My mouth separates as my tongue goes in search of his. Our tongues collide, ravenous for each other. Emotion suddenly rises in my chest and my breath hitches mid-kiss. Finn pulls back and his eyes search mine.

"What is it? Do you want me to stop?" he asks, his hands cupping my face.

"Don't stop. I want you. More than I ever knew I did."

His face relaxes, and the smirk that captivated me the first day I walked into O'Reilly's two years ago spreads across his face.

"You have no idea how long I've wanted this."

Finn's soft lips slowly take mine again as I regain my composure. He places kisses from the center of my collarbone down to my navel. Goosebumps follow his fingertips down both of my legs. I feel his lips on my ankle as my shoes disappear from my feet. Leaning up, I pull his shirt over his head, revealing the curves of his tight chest. He kisses my shoulder as he glides the straps of my romper down my arms and pushes it to my waist. The sweet torture continues as he nibbles on my neck while he one handedly unhooks and removes my bra. Gliding his touch across my collarbone to the place in between my breasts, he gently pushes me down. Restraint dwindles as he powerfully pulls the romper over my hips and tosses it to the floor. His greedy eyes rapidly take in my naked body as it moves with need.

Finn's massive hand runs over my skin before it lands in between my legs. Moving to my side, he takes my nipple into his warm wet mouth as he slides his fingers in. My teeth pull in my bottom lip as a growl emanates from deep in his throat. The wetness that was growing all night finally lets loose and covers him as he works in and out of me.

"Jesus, Daffodil," he breathes as his body descends, licking the entire way, eyes angled up at me. My breath picks up and my hands grip the sheets above my head. A moan slides out of my chest as his tongue hits me where his fingers just were, keeping good on his promise that his mouth would touch every part of me. It's difficult to keep my groans quiet as the emotion and satisfaction courses through my body. Failing miserably, I suddenly realize that it's my voice echoing in the room.

"Oh my God," I say as my hands pull so hard on the sheets behind my head, they rip out from underneath the mattress. Suddenly, Finn's mouth is gone and the heat of his body covers mine as I feel his tip entering. No longer in control of my own body, my head flings back as he fills me, and with a few thrusts, I convulse around him. My moans match his drives. My headboard thumps against the wall. Finn growls and buries himself deep inside of me as he gets the release he's been holding onto all night.

Once we both gain control of our breathing, Finn leans on one arm and he brushes the hair out of my face. The vision of him grinning down at me with that damned dimple could make me do or say anything. I've always known that I like Finnegan O'Reilly. But I never knew I loved him.

"I think my heart loves you," I blurt. Finally, I surrender to the need building inside for love. Even though I feel guilty for feeling it or wanting it. I'm also not prepared for Finn not to feel the same way. That's one of the reasons I didn't mean for this to come out now. Any fool would see he likes me. But love?

"Every single inch of me loves you and has for almost two years."

Happiness and relief only lasts for a second before what he just said sinks in. *He's loved me for almost two years?* Before I can say anything, he kisses my lips and then the heat from his body leaves me on a hiss, and he slowly walks to the bathroom. Lying there, staring at my ceiling, wondering if my neighbors heard every detail of the best sex I've ever had in my life, my heart is so full. But it's aching. *Two years.* Two years I could have had someone on my side, someone to hold me when I needed it, someone to love me when I was finding it difficult to love myself.

Sitting up, I turn to look at my bathroom door with the light glowing from under it. That man in there loves me and has for two years without me knowing it. The door opens, and he takes one look at me, then tilts his head to the side.

"What's wrong?" he asks quietly.

"I've wasted so much time. How do you not hate me for that? I threw myself at you twice. I took this away from us. The first time. I took that. It could have been like this, but I ruined that for us."

"No, you didn't," he says. "It's never been like this. This was the first time that I was able to have you exactly the way I always wanted you. It was the first time that love was in your eyes as I watched you give yourself to me. For the first time in two years, I can tell you I love you. You didn't ruin anything. You made it worth waiting for."

I've never known Finn to be a detailed talker. He's usually short with his words and gets his point across as quickly as possible. What he just said and how he said it, sends my heart straight over the edge. So much for playing this day-by-day and seeing how far it goes. I'm so far gone.

CHAPTER SIX

"IF YOU DO NOT STOP CALLING me at this time, I'm going to turn off my damn phone," I spit at Ryan.

He's called once again at nine o'clock in the morning.

"I didn't even notice the time, I swear. I just got to work and wanted to check up on you. Are you all right?"

"Yes, I'm fine. I don't know why you feel like you need to call me every day and ask me that."

Finn looks like he could jump through the phone. It wouldn't take much effort for Finn to annihilate Ryan. I take a deep calming breath and realize that I'm being too hard on Ryan. He's done nothing wrong other than annoy me. Not to mention, my anger really riles up Finn. Maybe it's just easy for me to take my anger out on Ryan instead of placing it where it should be. On myself.

"I didn't mean—"

"It's okay," I say. "I'm just tired. How are you doing? What's happening with the house?"

"I've been staying with Ally. It's been hard going in there, but I think I'm going to try to sleep there tonight." There's silence for a moment. "Are you going to sell it?"

My head tilts forward as a sigh escapes my chest. I wouldn't blame

Ryan if he never stepped foot into that house again and he doesn't have to. He has a good job that pays for him to travel. Now that Jarrod is gone, he isn't stuck in Albany anymore. He's talked about moving for years. It just makes me sad to put it up for sale knowing how proud Jarrod was of that house. With him gone now, the decision on what to do with the house rests on me. There aren't too many options for me though. I could never live there. The thought of living in Albany again is similar to the thought of being put in jail. Not to mentio the fact that I can hardly bear the thought of just walking into the front door. How can I not picture my brother on his last night? How Ryan is ever going to sleep there is beyond me.

"I guess I'll call a realtor that my family knows and we'll list it in a few weeks. Do you think that will give you enough time? We can always wait a little longer."

"Daphs—"

"Please, don't call me that."

Finn shifts on the bed next to me, and I can see the muscles working in his massive forearms as he tries to keep them planted on his legs. "You deserve so much credit for how much time you put into my brother's welfare. You tried as hard as I did. I feel badly that your life is changing so drastically."

"You're the reason. You know that, right? You are the only reason Jarrod didn't leave us sooner. He was always so worried about you. He made me promise, that if one day he wasn't here anymore, that I would look out for you." Ryan's voice softens to a whisper, "I promised him."

That sounds exactly like something Jarrod would have said. It makes total sense now why Ryan is calling me all the time suddenly and coming to Boston to check out my hangouts and my apartment. He's trying to keep his promise.

"As long as you aren't a complete dick, I won't make you break that promise. Listen, I've got to go. I'm sure I'll talk to you again soon. Tell Ally I said hi."

"Will do, Daphs. Later."

My eyes roll at the nickname that I only seemed to tolerate from Jarrod. "Later."

Glad that conversation is over, I slide back down under the covers. There's still time before we have to get up so I shut my eyes, but Finn isn't moving from his sitting position next to me. Through a squinted eye, I see his muscles still haven't relaxed either.

Huffing, I sit back up and lean into him. "I know you have a weird feeling about Ryan, but I'm telling you, he's harmless."

Finn's face turns abruptly toward me. "I'm not worried about that jackass."

"Then what is it?"

"I should have seen that you were goin' through so much shit. What you were dealing with was intense and I could have been easier on you at work. I can't imagine goin' through all that shit without havin' anyone to lean on yourself. I just assumed you had a man and I was a sidepiece. That was my stupid mistake."

"The only reason you thought I had a man was because I allowed you to think that way. Over the years, I got really good at hiding my personal life from everyone. I had Leigh; she helped."

"It ain't the same. I'm glad you had a friend, but it isn't the same as having someone to help take some of that pressure off and help you forget for just a little while."

"Well, you're here now."

"That, you can fuckin' count on. And I'm not goin' anywhere."

My hand touches his loosening arm as I lean over and kiss his cheek. The dimple appears on the side of his face and I quickly plant a kiss on it before it disappears again. His head turns to catch my mouth, quickly pressing a kiss into my lips. I sink further into the covers, still tired, and yawn loudly. Pulling on Finn's arm, I try to convince him to relax and go back to sleep, knowing damn well I am not moving this man unless he wants to be moved. The bed shifts as he lowers himself back down. I wrap my leg over his and my arm over his torso. His hand rests comfortably on top of mine. The warmth from his cheek rests against my forehead. Being folded into Finn, it feels like I'm exactly where I'm supposed to be.

Though my heart is still sad and a piece of it will always be missing, what once was a black hole is now beating pure red love.

* * *

"FUCK THESE GOD DAMNED PHONES," Finn sneers as I sleepily sit up, rubbing my eyes. "Kael better have a good fuckin' reason for callin'... Oh, hey there, Firecracker." The change in Finn's voice brings a smile to my face. Settling back into the covers, I listen to Finn talk to one of his favorite people in this world. Sophie and Finn have a special bond. One that blood couldn't have made closer. There's no doubt Finn still blames himself for shit that went down last year with Sophie. I see it in his eyes every time my fingertips touch his scars. Pain, but not the physical kind. I heard Kael ask him one time if he was still having nightmares, so I know that at least for a while after the incident, it tormented him. Sophie is fine now, but there are times when I get the feeling that Finn isn't completely fine.

"I can ask her," Finn says. He turns to me as he moves the phone away from his mouth. "They want us to come to dinner this weekend. Benson's got business in town, so they'll be here for a few days."

"Sure," I agree quickly. Finn squints his eyes as if he's analyzing me. "Really, I think it would be fun. I like Sophie."

He shrugs before turning back to the phone. "Just let me know what I can bring—yeah, I know we have this argument every time we have dinner. For fuck's sake woman, it's not like it's a big deal for me to bring some damn beers or sodas."

"I can bring a dessert," I spurt out. Finn turns and gives me a surprised look.

"You bake, Daffodil?"

"What? Is that so hard to believe?"

"Daphne says she'll bring the dessert. Oh, for cryin' out loud." I turn to Finn to expect his face to be irritated but instead see a kind smile across his face. "That sounds good, Firecracker. You need me, call."

"She doesn't want me to bring a dessert?"

"Surprisingly, she didn't argue on you bringin' dessert one bit."

"Then why did you say 'for crying out loud'?"

"She started to give me shit about you havin' a nickname. It slipped my mind that I hadn't told her."

"I still don't think that nickname even fits me. I don't have the same disposition as a bright and cheery yellow flower," I snicker and move to get out of the bed.

"You're wrong." The sound of his voice makes my body halt. Finn moves close to my back and pushes my hair to the side, revealing my shirt has fallen off my shoulder. "Daffodils can bloom even through the coldest days. Even through snow. They are hardy, bold, and strong, yet feminine and delicate." His lips touch the curve of my shoulder, then he places a kiss closer to my neck. "You are every bit a fuckin' daffodil."

"I'm not strong. Most of the time I feel absolutely defeated." Strength is an attribute that I've faked my entire life. I've never told a soul how some days the weakness eats at my insides. Yet in this moment, the truth comes flowing out. Turning me, he again places his finger under my chin and lifts my lowered head so that our eyes meet. Immediately regretting making myself so vulnerable, I stand tall quickly and back away. "Can we stop talking about this? We have to get ready for work anyways." Finn's eyebrows furrow with worry, but he nods. Trying to ease him, I flash a quick smile then hurry to the bathroom for a shower.

As usual, I look for Herman to be camped out right outside the bathroom door after I've finished showering. I smile as he bolts in the room. Before I can look up to see where I'm going, I run right into Finn. His hands rest on the upper portion of both of my arms. Looking up into his determined eyes, I'm not sure what to expect.

"You may not feel strong sometimes, but the proof of your true strength is you standing here right in front of me. And if you should ever weaken, I'll be here to hold you up until your strength returns. You got that?"

Stunned and lacking the ability to respond, I nod.

"Good. I'm goin' to run home and clean up. I'll meet you at the pub. Love you, Daffodil." His warm wet lips enclose on mine with a deep kiss.

"I love you, too," I can only whisper. I've never had this. I've never had someone willing to hold me up when I can't stand, and it takes my breath away.

* * *

As THE LAST customer leaves O'Reilly's for the night, I rush to get my cleanup done. The past week was filled with busy nights lead by the distractions of Finn and his wandering hands in the hallway of the pub. Other than getting pulled into his office a few times for a few quick kisses, we've hardly spent any time alone together. Working with Finn is more difficult now than ever before. Now I can actually touch him whenever I want to. And I want to. All the time. Even though we have a hard time keeping our hands off of each other, Finn still has to run the pub.

Dinner with Benson and Sophie tomorrow should be fun. But I can't stop the anxiety that's building as the time gets closer. Working with Sophie was always easy, though she usually kept to herself. She wasn't one to start a conversation, but if you did, she was great to talk to. We always got along and shared a few quick laughs here and there. But this is different than just being a fellow co-worker. I'm going as Finn's date. It's not the same anymore.

I'm trying to push those worries out of my head and remember that this dinner will be a good way to focus on living my life how I always wished it could be. I've decided to bring a Better Than Sex cake, although I hardly think that's an accurate name. It should be named Almost Better Than Sex But Not Quite cake.

A slow and gentle touch wraps around the small of my back as his breath on my shoulder releases of a shiver. "Are you finished?" he asks.

"I just need to cash out," I whisper.

"Good. I've about gone crazy this week. I'm coming to your place tonight."

"Are we ever going to your place?"

"Not unless you want Kael to know how you sound when I make you come undone. You aren't real quiet."

As hard as I try to be quiet, Finn makes it impossible. He brings out a side of me that isn't in control of my own body or voice. One I didn't even realize I had. He's right. If Kael heard me I'm not sure I could ever look him in the eyes again.

"Point taken. My place."

With the last punch on the keyboard officially clocking me out, he lifts me up and flings me over his shoulder.

"Put me down," I shout. His shoulder shakes under my belly. The asshole is laughing at me. Kael walks past and shakes his head.

"Finnegan O'Reilly. You put me down before I kick your ass."

"Not a chance, Daffodil. You take too long walkin' and I've been thinkin' about you all week. Seeing you all night struttin' around my bar without being able to have you is making me fuckin' nuts. I'm not riskin' you takin' any more time."

Finn laughs harder as a loud sigh comes from my chest. As we exit the pub and walk around the corner, the beep of Finn's Wrangler echoes against the buildings. He playfully smacks my ass, making me giggle, then he opens the passenger door and places me in the seat. He leans in, hovering over me. His hand reaches up and grabs my cheek as he takes my mouth hard and fast. My hands drift forcefully around his head. The need to feel him against my skin becomes overwhelming. Finn grunts as he pulls away from me and quickly slams my door, then hustles to the driver's seat.

"Are you grunting at me?" I tease.

Finn's dimple gets deep as he flashes me a seductive side smile. "Don't worry. You'll be grunting soon."

I immediately feel the warmth between my legs. Trying to focus out of the window, I shake my head smiling. When we pull up to my apartment, Finn stops in the road right in front. I look to him, puzzled.

"You go in. Greet your damn cat. Maybe you'll be done with that shit by the time I park and come up."

I quickly hop out, and as my foot hits the first step on my stoop, Finn floors the gas on the Wrangler. His eagerness makes me laugh. I unlock the door to the building quickly. Grabbing a piece of paper from my purse, I stick it between the door and the frame so that Finn doesn't get locked out. Then I rush up the stairs to my apartment.

Like clockwork, Herman comes running as soon as the door opens. My hands are full of black soft fur when the door to my apartment opens and Finn comes in. He locks the door behind him and holds his hand out to me to help me off of the floor. Wasting no time, his hands grab the hem of my shirt and lift it swiftly over my head. Not wanting to be the only one exposed, I grab the hem of his shirt and try to lift it over his head, but I struggle to get it over his head even on my tip toes. Finn flashes me a grin as one hand goes over his head and grabs the back of his shirt, then smoothly lifts it over his head. Just the way he took off his damn shirt makes me melt.

Wild and desperate hands strip any clothes remaining between us. The scent of aged oak and whiskey accompanies my deep inhale as I place my lips against his neck. As my lips part, my tongue slowly travels down his neck. A hiss leaves his mouth as he plants his hands on my ass and lifts me up. My legs wrap around his torso as he moves swiftly toward the bedroom. The anticipation and moans build intensely with each step as the tip of him presses ever so slightly into me.

"Finn," I pant into his ear as I suck in the lower part of his earlobe.

With one hand he eases us onto the bed. His lips are relentless against me as he moves them all over my skin. I'm about to beg, when he pulls my nipple into his mouth and the only thing I can get out is a whispered, "Yes". My hips begin to rock, needy for him. As he leans back, his seductive, dimpled grin makes my heart beat faster. My bottom lip makes a squeak as I suck it in when Finn pushes his fingers into me. My back lifts from the bed as he works me. Lacking the will power and the ability to last any longer, I sit up, put my hand on his chest, and push him to the bed. With a leg on either side of him, I gently guide him into me. Our slow motions only last a moment before Finn's hands grip my hips and his fingers dig in as he helps me bounce on him.

"Oh, damn," he whispers.

My moans and breath get quicker as I near release. To steady myself, I place my hands on Finn's chest as the wave of my climax hits me. The muscles on the inside of my legs shake and I lose my momentum to the power of it. With little effort, Finn flips us and takes over. His thrusts are rhythmic until he places his hand on my chest. He pushes in slowly and with a guttural groan as he reaches his climax.

We both rest on our backs, neither wanting to get up yet. Finn's eyes are closed as his thumb moves back and forth over my skin. But my vision is drawn to his scar on his chest. My fingertips skim over the lightened pigmentation. I glance at his face, and there it is. That deep pain within him. He grabs my hand and kisses it, then moves it to his stomach.

"I know you are still having a hard time with what happened."

Oh God. Why did I just say that out loud?

"Stop." His voice gentle but warning as he presses his lips against my neck. But I can't stop. This is probably the worst timing in the world, but I can't stop seeing the pain that appears in his eyes when I touch him there.

"You can talk to me."

"Enough!"

I jump at the harsh tone in his voice.

He looks at me and it's obvious that I've crossed a line. Even though I'm a little hurt, the anger is greater. I've poured my heart out to Finn. Shared everything with him that I kept secret for so long. His eyes follow me as I finally snatch my shirt from the floor and stomp into the bathroom.

The bath water is already turning cool, but instead of getting out, I just turn on the hot water again. I'm not even sure that Finn is still in my apartment. The anger has faded and anxiety has replaced it. How can I give so much of myself to Finn, when he obviously isn't ready to give me the same?

"Can I come in?" Finn's voice is low and coming from a small crack in the bathroom door.

"Yes."

The door swings open, Finn marches in, then takes a seat on the lid

71

of the toilet. His elbows on his knees and hands clasped, he stares into me.

"I don't want to talk about it. It bothers me that it bothers you, but it's over and I'm not talking about it anymore."

"Then I guess you can go."

Finn's face twists. "Go? I'm not goin' anywhere."

"I've been through hell with someone close to me that refused to tell me when things were bad until it was too late. I won't live through that again."

"It's not like that…"

"I don't want just bits and pieces of you. If this is going to work, I want everything."

His face turns away. "Just like you, I don't want to relive it. I'm fine. I swear." As the cool air from the living room filters into the bathroom, my skin prickles with goosebumps. "Come on, Daffodil. You're cold."

Finn grabs the towel from the hook on the wall and holds it out for me. I pull the drain and step out of the tub into Finn's arms. The chill only lasts for a second before he wraps me up tightly. His lips press against my forehead. As much as I don't like it, I'm trying to understand.

"I love you, Daffodil."

"I love you, too."

After pulling on an old rolling stone T-shirt, I climb into bed next to Finn. My mind races about our dinner tomorrow. Sitting at a table with people Finn considers his family won't be easy.

Two powerful arms reach over and pull me into his side. He doesn't say anything, but his finger goes under my chin to lift my face to his. His beautiful blue eyes meet mine before he places a kiss on my lips. He lowers his finger and smiles at me. I know he wants me to believe that he's fine. I return his smile, but that doesn't mean that I don't see the pang of hurt in his eyes.

CHAPTER SEVEN

EARLY IN OUR FRIENDSHIP, Leigh learned how much I love baking. Since I can't eat everything I make, I always bring some to Leigh. Her son Landon loves brownies, so I make those a lot. And cupcakes, because who doesn't love a cupcake? The first time I brought Leigh treats, she returned my container with a perfectly folded apron sitting inside with a note attached.

Saw you had flour all over your pretty black top. This will help with that. Thank you for the treats.

The apron is the opposite of what I would have picked out. Black is my usual first choice with red as my second. But Leigh being Leigh, gave me one with pink straps and is covered in colorful cupcakes with glitter on the frosting. It's completely against everything I stand for in clothing. However, I wear it proudly and have come to love putting it on while I bake. It's a good thing I have it on today. The kitchen is a wreck. Messy spatulas, dirty bowls, and flour covering the kitchen counter.

"Hey, what's going on out here?" Finn asks as he comes out of the bedroom, yawning and rubbing his eyes. His mouth drops as he opens his eyes.

"I didn't mean to wake you, but shit starts goin' down when I bake," I giggle. What I'm not going to tell him is how my brain won't stop worrying. How I wasn't thinking about the cake when I flipped the switch on my mixer after I dumped all the flour in. It was like a flour explosion in here. I had to clean that all up once already and start all over again.

Quickly moving around the kitchen, I begin to clean up my mess even though there's more to do. I still have to make the pudding part that you pour over the cake when it comes out of the oven. It takes me a minute to see that Finn still hasn't moved from his place in the doorway of the bedroom.

"Why are you looking at me like that?"

"I…it…you…*fuck*. So many reasons." Both of his hands go up to his head and rub back and forth as the addictive smile I love spreads across his face. He walks to me and brushes off some of the flour that made its way up to my cheek. I'm a freaking mess in the kitchen on a normal day. I love to bake, but I would pay someone a lot of money to come and clean this shit up when I'm done.

"It smells so good in here." Finn kisses me, then turns away and walks back toward the bedroom.

"Hey, where are you going?"

"If I look at you too much longer in that cute ass apron, your cake is gonna burn."

Finn disappears into the bedroom for a few minutes, then comes out with his clothes from yesterday on.

"I gotta get out of here before I can't control my hands anymore. I'm goin' to head to my house to get clean clothes and make sure Kael is all set at the pub for tonight. I'll be back around four, and we'll head over to Benson and Sophie's."

Before he walks out the door, he kisses me, bends down to scratch Herman's head, then angles his head back at me. His dimple is the last thing I see on his way out.

Thankfully, the cake comes out perfect, which slightly settles my nerves. There's nothing worse than when you need something to turn out well and it sucks. I've showered and picked out my nicest black skinny jeans, sans rips, and a collared white sleeveless blouse with a pair of flats. My hair is backcombed by the crown with a braid running across the front of my head which is then pulled into a ponytail in the back. It's still very much my style but cleaned up a bit. I haven't lost all of that prim and proper etiquette. The last time I went to dinner at someone else's house was years ago. Hopefully, the outfit I chose won't be too casual or too fancy.

I'm in the middle of opening a can of cat food for Herman when the bell goes off that someone is downstairs. I press the button and let them up, then unlock my apartment door. Finn comes in with an agitated glare.

"What the hell is wrong with you?" I ask.

"Do you have any idea how dangerous it is for you to just buzz someone in? What if it wasn't me?" he scolds.

"It's four, which is when you said you would be coming, and it is you, soo…" I laugh and put my hands up in the air.

"It's not funny, Daphne."

I jerk my face back at the sound of my real name coming out of his mouth. After our little argument last night, I'm feeling a bit on edge.

"You can't just buzz someone in the building. That's what these little things are made for," he says while pointing at the intercom that I apparently should have used.

"Okay, geez."

"C'mon. We need to go. The last thing I want to deal with today is Firecracker bein' a damn firecracker about me bein' late."

With the cake in my hands, Finn takes one look at it, then looks back at me with a smirk and shakes his head as he holds the door open. I take this as a sign that he's over being angry at my lack of security concerns. My phone starts ringing in my purse when we are halfway down the stairs, but I let it go to voicemail. Finn is right here and sadly, there isn't anyone else that I would need to answer the phone for. Not anymore. Once we get into the Wrangler, I place the cake on my lap and dig into my purse, pulling out my phone. I click the phone off just as quickly as I clicked it on and toss it back into my purse. There's no way I'm calling Ryan back right now. Ryan has been calling me every day. Most days he calls numerous times, but I only answer once. I'm sure living in the house that he shared with my brother is excruciating for him. I think he has a trip coming up for work soon, so hopefully that will help to get him out of my hair for a while. I'm trying to be nicer to Ryan, though he is egocentric and apparently the world should now revolve around him. I'm sure he'll be calling me again soon anyway.

We pull up to a beautiful tall glass building. My mouth hangs open as a man in a sharp black suit opens my door to assist me out. I look questioning to Finn.

"Benson's building has valet parking."

"I know what valet is, thank you," I say, snarky. "I just didn't realize this is one of Benson's buildings."

Finn comes around the vehicle as he passes his keys to the valet. He grabs my elbow since my hands are holding the cake and walks alongside of me into the building. No one asks our name or which apartment we are going to. Instead, everyone just nods and smiles at us. Large windows take up most of the wall space in every direction in the lobby. The floors are shiny white and gray marble, and I love the clicking our shoes make as we walk to the farthest elevator. The door opens, and we step inside, but there are no floor buttons to press. There's only a keypad. Finn quickly taps in a five-digit code, the doors close, and we start to ascend. All the way to the top floor. An open foyer greets us with a beautiful arrangement of flowers on a large round table. On the opposite side of that is a large white door. Finn knocks, and it only takes seconds before Sophie opens the door and about knocks Finn over as she hugs him so tightly.

"Hey. Can't breathe," he says, joking to Sophie.

"I've missed you."

"You just talked to me on the phone yesterday." He gives her another squeeze before releasing her and stepping into the condo. Sophie turns to me with a big friendly smile, and she pushes her long brown hair behind her shoulder.

"It's so nice to see you, Daphne. How are you? It's been a long time since I've been in the pub. Here, let me take that for you." She grabs the cake from my hands and nods with her head to motion me into the condo.

"I'm good. Thanks for having me over. Your place is beautiful."

The condo is gorgeous. Almost everything is white, but there's a warmness to the space that evens the atmosphere. Most of the warmth coming from the earth-toned furniture. I admire a gorgeous painting of a mountain scene hanging as the main focus in the living room where deep green accents compliment it. The condo features clean modern lines, yet it's warm and inviting. I'm not sure how she accomplished that, but I love it. The view of the harbor is breathtaking out of the large floor to ceiling windows in the living room.

After a few minutes of being swept up in the beauty that surrounds me, I realize that I've been entranced. I look around for Finn, but he's disappeared and Sophie is standing next to me with a cup of tea.

"Finn said you like tea. I hope you like black tea."

"Thank you, I love black tea."

"C'mon and have a seat. Finn and Benson will be out in a little while, I'm sure. Those two are ridiculous," she says as she smiles and shakes her head. Suddenly, I hear yelling from the other room and I look puzzled in that direction.

"Don't worry. They're playing video games. It's the dumbest thing I've ever seen, but they have fun so who am I to criticize? It's fascinating how the two of them can turn into large children over a game."

"I didn't even know Finn played video games."

"Benson started playing since he's been working less. He sort of pulled Finn into it. With so much to do at the pub, he rarely has time to do anything else." Her faces blushes a bit, a sly smile sliding across her face. "Well, he obviously found some time to do something else, but it wasn't video games."

Even though Sophie looks relaxed and comfortable on her couch, I couldn't feel less that way. I know Sophie, but it's different being in her home and as a guest of Finn. I'm trying everything to relax, but I can't help but feel like I'm meeting Finn's family for the first time.

"Listen," Sophie hesitates. "I want you to know that Finn told me about your brother."

My body freezes and I choke a bit on my tea. I'm not sure if I'm angry that Finn told Sophie about my brother or if I'm just sad that this is going to be part of my story for the rest of my life.

"He told me because he tells me everything. He tells me things that he doesn't tell his own brother. I don't want you to be angry with him because he didn't say it just to be telling me your business. He had some shit he needed to work out in himself and what he was feeling. Please don't be hard on him about it. I'm also not going to bring it up again, unless you want to talk about it. I'm sure you have friends, but if you ever need to talk about anything, I'm always available. I only had to tell you that I know because I feel like it would be fake of me to pretend that I didn't."

I know that Sophie and Finn have a special bond. I would never question that or be jealous that he tells her everything. But I also can't help to be hurt that he can give that someone but not to me. Sitting here, I know that I have a decision to make. Either I accept Finn for who he is and be patient until he feels like he can talk to me the same way, or I walk away. The thought of putting an end to the years I've loved Finn make my heart sink. I guess it's decided. I'm not walking away.

"I appreciate that. Thank you. I'm still a bit numb about it all."

A faint cry comes from the other room, and Sophie starts to rise from the couch.

"I've got her," Finn yells into the living room from the back. Sophie smiles, grabs her coffee, and sits back down. Benson walks into the living room with the same big white smile he wears when he walks into the pub.

"Hi, Daphne. How are you?" he asks as he leans down and kisses my cheek like a proper gentleman. I've seen Benson a number of times in the pub. However, the only conversation I've had with him was his drink order. He comes in whenever he is in town to visit with Finn, Kael, and Paul.

"I'm good, thanks."

Benson moves to Sophie and plants a sweet kiss on her lips. "I'm going to check on dinner," he announces as he leaves the room.

Movement coming from the hallway catches my eyes. My body freezes as I lock in on Finn and his huge arms holding a little girl. His face is buried in her neck, and she giggles the best belly laugh I've ever heard. He flashes me a sweet smile, and then heads into the kitchen with Sophie and Benson's daughter, Katie, tucked firmly into his arm. Her little hand grasps the back of his shoulder. Once he's completely out of view, I turn back to Sophie who is staring at me.

"There is nothing quite like seeing the man you love with a baby is there?" Her devious smile is one that would rival Leigh's.

"I never pictured Finn with a baby before, but now seeing him, he looks so natural."

Sophie grins. "I pity her when she gets older. I'm not sure I'm going to be able to help her. Between Benson, Finn, Kael, and Paul, they'll be chasing all the boys away."

"Oh no, those boys have no chance," I agree.

"What about you?" she asks me.

"Me?"

"Do you want kids someday?"

"I've never thought about it." I hesitate, but she knows all about Jarrod so there's no reason to hold back. "My entire life revolved around my brother. I never thought I would have the time to have my own life. Truthfully, I don't know how I feel about it yet."

"Dinner's done, ladies," Benson calls.

Sophie smiles. "Don't worry. Life has a way of figuring things out for you." She taps my knee, and we both rise from the couch and go to the dining room to join our men and Katie. Finn has placed her in a high chair next to him. I take the seat on the other side and get real excited about the steak and potatoes that are on the table.

As the conversations flow throughout dinner, the anxiety melts away. It's as if the four of us have been friends for years. I don't feel out of place once, and it feels good. Really good. After we have all finished, I help Sophie with the dishes. Once everything is cleaned up from dinner, we bring out the cake.

Finn devours his piece and gets another one. Katie has cake all over her face and I'm pretty sure on the wall too. Finn laughs as he gently wipes her face with a tiny napkin in his massive hands.

"This is amazing. We should sell this at the pub. I bet people would go nuts."

"Oh, quit. It's such an easy recipe, anybody could make it."

"Nope. I've had this kind of cake before, and it wasn't this good," Sophie says.

Smiling, the heat rises in my cheeks. This is just one of the reasons I love baking. It's therapeutic in a way for me, but I always hoped it could make others feel happy. It finally feels like I was able do that.

Back in the living room, the five of us sit around, mainly being entertained by Katie. At one point, she teeters over to me and raises her hands for me to pick her up. I play with her for a few minutes before she is done with me and wants her uncle again. Finn keeps my attention all night, even though I try not to make it obvious that I am taking every opportunity I can to stare at him with Katie. Seeing him with a baby girl is doing something to me. The way he can make her giggle, the way he holds her, and the way she clings to him. Eventually, she nuzzles onto his massive chest and falls asleep as he rubs her back. The entire damn scene is enough to make me fall in love with him if I wasn't already. He stands, holding her protectively as Sophie stands to take her from him.

"Don't you dare," he whispers to her. "You get to do it every night. Let me put my niece to bed."

Sophie leans in and kisses her babies forehead as I hear her whisper, "Goodnight, my sweet girl."

As soon as Finn returns from putting Katie to bed, he looks to me. "You ready to go, Daffodil?"

I nod and turn to Sophie. "Thank you so much for having me."

"Of course. It was such a fun night. I hope we can do it again soon." Then she leans in close while the guys are chatting as they walk toward the door. "I mean it. If you ever want to talk, please call me. Get my number from Finn's phone and program it. Call me anytime. Hey, maybe you guys could come to the mountain house sometime for a weekend if Finn can ever pull himself away from the pub for that long."

"That would be awesome. I've heard so much about the place. Thanks again."

Sophie envelopes me in her arms as though we've been close friends for years. Benson gives me a gentle hug with a formal kiss on the cheek goodbye. As the door to the foyer shuts behind us, Finn grabs my hand and pulls it up to his mouth, kissing it before leading us back to the elevator.

* * *

"What are we doing here?" I ask confused as Finn pulls the Wrangler up to a parking lot that faces the water. The lights of the city buildings dance on the surface.

"Thought we'd take in the city for a bit."

I nod and let a few minutes pass without saying anything.

"Holding that baby fits you," I say.

"I've only held a baby one other time in my life before Katie. I was nervous, felt like I didn't know what I was doing, and honestly, I hated it. I have never once felt that way with Katie. The day she was born, she fit perfectly right into my arms. I never knew love like that before. It was instant." He breathes deeply. "Where do you see yourself in a few years?"

My palms instantly get sweaty. "I don't know. I thought my life had been planned out for me and that I would have my brother to take care of. I never considered even having a boyfriend, much less anything more than that. So I guess, I just want whatever feels right. I'm just flying with the wind."

"I think that's a good plan."

Finn puts his arm over the console and situates his hand in the crook of my knee. I snuggle up his arm and feel completely content just being here with him. Suddenly, I realize that I've been tracing the barely there scars on his arm. Quickly, I retract them, as I don't want to fight with Finn after the nice evening we've had.

"That was one of the worst days of my life. The way Sophie was bleeding... her expression as she watched me go down, still haunts me. I haven't had a nightmare in a few months, but they used to be almost every night. I've gotten to a point where I can say that I'm fine. But it will always be part of me, just like these damn scars. I didn't follow my gut. I knew something didn't seem right but let my guard down anyway. It was my fault that I left her alone in that house. Then I couldn't save her. I was useless."

This was the last thing I was expecting tonight. I had come to terms with Finn not wanting to talk about it anymore. My heart is both soaring and ripping in half.

"I could tell you it wasn't your fault all night long. But I know how that goes. Other people's words are quieter than the ones that you tell yourself. At some point, you have to forgive yourself. Sophie is alive and happy. And so are you. That's all that matters anymore."

"No. All that matters to me anymore, is you. When I saw you with Katie tonight, I couldn't help but remember how fragile this all is."

I nod, knowing exactly what he means. He leans over again and kisses me. We sit for a while with the windows down, holding hands, and enjoying the view before going home.

"You're not coming up?" I ask him, as he pulls up to the front of my building.

"I want to, but I have to run to the pub for a while. There's some paperwork I have to do and I can't say how long it's going to take me. I'll call you tomorrow."

I flash a playful pouty lip which gets me a chuckle. He cups my face with his hand and presses a deep kiss on my lips.

"Go take care of business," I say before getting out of the Jeep. As I let myself in the door of my building, I see that Finn is still in the street and watches me until the door is completely shut before he takes off.

I pull out my cellphone, which I silenced during dinner because it wouldn't stop ringing. The phone powers up and there are a dozen missed calls. I'm alarmed as some of them are from Leigh. My feet quicken their pace climbing the stairs to get to Leigh's apartment. As I reach the top of the stairs, it's clear why she had been calling me all night. A certain annoying man is sitting against my door, a bottle of whiskey in one hand and a paper of some kind in the other. My shoulders sink as I look to the sky and ask why this is happening to me. This was not how I planned on spending the rest of this great day. Lowering my head, I take a deep breath trying to will myself the patience I need to speak.

"What are you doing here, Ryan?"

His head bounces between his shoulders and my front door as he tries to look at me. Then he raises the hand with the paper in my direction until I take it from him. He takes another long swig from the bottle. Before I'm able to look at the paper Ryan handed me, Leigh comes bouncing out of her door.

"Oh, good. You're here. I tried calling you to warn you he was here and that he isn't in good shape. I wasn't sure if you wanted me to let him in or not, so I just let him chill here and kept checking on him. He's quite inebriated," she says, lifting her eyebrows and looking down at him.

"Help me get him inside, will you?"

She nods and I shove the paper into my purse. Between the two of us giving it all we've got, we barely get him in the door of my apartment. Even Herman knows something is up because I look for him as we open the door and he isn't coming out. We leave Ryan on the floor just inside the door. He lifts the bottle up to his lips, but I rip it out of his hand. Not because I give a shit if he's drunk, that's his problem. But when he shows up at my apartment and now I have to take care of him, that's my problem.

"I've got it from here," I tell Leigh. "Thanks for watching out for him, although I'm not sure what to do with him now."

"Well, good luck," she says as she walks out the door.

The slam of my purse on the kitchen counter doesn't even phase him. I lean against the counter, just staring at Ryan who is already passed out right there on my fucking floor. I step over him and go into the bathroom to remove my makeup and take down my hair before changing into yoga capris and an off-the-shoulder comfy gray t-shirt.

My only defense is to climb into bed and pray that I can fall asleep quickly so that the anger and annoyance doesn't eat at me. After lying here for what seems like an hour, I remember that Ryan handed me something that quickly got shoved into my purse. It could wait until the morning. But it's much earlier than my normal bedtime anyway. Giving in to curiosity, I get the paper from my purse and bring it back into my bed. The minute I see the writing on the front of an envelope, I wish I never even touched it. I drop it and cover my face as if that will shield me from the absolute grief that will be inside. Not knowing how I'm going to open it, I stare at those five letters through parted fingers. Jarrod's handwriting. *Daphs.*

CHAPTER EIGHT

IT BECOMES PAINFULLY clear why Ryan came to Boston and why he's drunk. He probably got one of these, too. One of these horrible letters that I'm sure Jarrod left as a way to comfort us. However, it feels as though my insides are being put through a paper shredder. Most of my brain is telling me not to open this letter. Nothing inside of it is going to make this better. Nothing inside of it is going to make me feel like it's okay to be moving on with my life. Against all of my better judgment, I peel back the seal with trembling fingers and remove the folded paper inside. My cheeks become wet, and my breath is removed from my lungs as I see his handwriting all over the page.

MY DEAREST DAPHS,

If this should ever get to you, I'm so sorry. I just couldn't find the light anymore, and I'm tired of the dark. I feel like a prisoner in my own body. Don't be like me. Be strong. Be courageous. Be a risk taker. Most of all, be happy. I could never do any of those things. I'm well aware of the sacrifices you have made for me. It was never fair to you. If you are reading this, I'm free, and so are you. I hope you have a happy and delightfully messy life. I'll love you always, even in death.

-Jarrod

THE SOBS COME HARD and long. I wish I had never read it. The only thing I hear other than my hiccupped breaths is Ryan's drunken snoring. Leaving the note on my bed, I put on my shoes and run out of my apartment and into the street. The outdoor air hits my lungs like needle pricks. Suddenly, I realize that I'm heading to the only person I want to see right now. The person who unexpectedly has become my solace.

As I walk into the pub, Kael sees me from behind the bar. I take a short step back as he jumps over the bar and rushes toward me, his face looking scary.

"What's the matter? What happened?" His body bulks up as he grabs onto my elbow, protectively pulling me into him and scanning behind me.

"I just need to see Finn," I whisper.

"You're shaking. Did someone hurt you?"

"No."

"Is someone following you?"

"No. I just need Finn."

"Here, sit down and I'll go find him. You need a water?" He leads me to a booth, and I sit just to appease him. My legs bounce under the table because I'm unable to keep them still.

"No water."

Kael nods and turns to go back to the office, but before he reaches the entrance to the hallway, a waitress calls him to a table that is being rowdy. He looks back to me holding up one finger to indicate that he'll only be one minute, but I'm not waiting on Kael, so I get up and head to the back. The office door is closed, but Finn always told me to just come in, so I turn the handle. As soon as the door is fully open, it's like I'm punched right in the gut. My mouth drops, my eyes widen, and my feet begin to move back out of the office.

"Daffodil," he yells, but I can barely hear it as my running feet already have me out of the front door of the pub.

Once outside, I keep running. I know he's going to come after me, so I hail a taxi and have him take me to the closest liquor store. The driver agrees to wait for me while I'm inside grabbing the first bottle of liquor I can find. I ask him to take me to the park. After assuring the driver that I'll be fine at night by myself on the Harborwalk, I pay him and wave as I start walking along the path. It's my favorite part of Boston at night. Once I reach my usual spot, I place my legs under the heavy chain that lines the walk and place my arms over it so I don't fall into the water below. The night sky is lit up by the orange hue of the city. My eyes are transfixed by the dancing lights on the water from the buildings of the Financial District across Boston Harbor. The sound of the water splashing against the concrete below my feet isn't loud enough to silence the pain surging through me. This late at night, there may be a passerby or two but not many. I twist open my bottle of vodka and chug. I have every intention of drinking away the sight of Finn sitting face-to-face with another woman in his office. They were holding hands. The same hands that were just holding mine while he confessed his love for me. My eyes burn as tears flow from them.

As sad as it is to say, my brother's death wasn't all that shocking. I had hoped that it would never happen, but the two suicide attempts in the past made it a reality that he could try again. He did, and this time, he succeeded. My heart has yet to recover from that—and now, Finn's pure and brutal betrayal. That was one I didn't see coming. I wasn't sure my heart could be any more broken than it was the night my brother died. Tonight, I realized it could.

The only good thing about my childhood was that it has made me strong. I might be sad, but I'm going to be all right. Life is going to go on. Thinking about my brother, my parents, Finn and Ryan, maybe I should move. Start an entirely new life, somewhere new and exciting. I have nothing holding me back now. I could move across the country and go wherever I want to go. I have the money. As these thoughts continue to flutter through my mind, the sky begins to brighten with yellows and oranges. My drunken buzz wore off a few hours ago. Feet pad heavily behind me on the trail as the early risers start their runs. When someone passes me on their cellphone saying "I love you" to whomever is on the other end, I stand up, take one more look out to the water, and decide that I've about fucking had it. I'm going to my apartment, kicking Ryan's dumbass out, and packing my shit.

The taxi ride home is quiet. I begin to make a mental list of all the places I could live. I'll have to pick one if I'm going. All my intentions are to get into my apartment and pack as fast as I can, so I can take off. So I run from the second I get out of that taxi until I hit my front door. But before I can get inside, Leigh comes at me.

"Where the hell have you been?" she screeches.

"I went down to the harbor. Why?"

"Oh, Jesus. You seriously have no clue, do you?"

"What?" I ask, annoyed.

"Everyone is out searching for you. They're calling me nonstop to see if you've come home. Finn is worried sick."

"Oh, did you talk to Finn? Did he tell you what happened?" I ask her, crossing my arms.

"No, he just said you were upset and took off."

"Of course he didn't," I say, then sigh. "I got a letter that Jarrod wrote before he died and I was upset."

Leigh covers her mouth with her hand.

"I went to the pub because I just wanted to be with Finn and tell him about the letter. But when I walked into the office, he was having a pretty intimate moment with another woman. He obviously dropped me off last night for a reason."

"That son of bitch," Leigh yelled. "I can't believe he would do that to you. Men are such assholes sometimes."

Leigh's words from earlier peak my curiosity. "Who is everyone?"

"Finn, Kael, Benson, Paul, and Ryan."

I sigh heavily. I can't believe he even got Benson and Paul into this mess. They need to know that I'm okay so that they can all go home.

"Will you do me a favor?" I ask, and Leigh nods. "Call Finn and tell him that you've seen me and I'm fine, but I'm not at home. Tell him I came home, packed a bag, and left."

"You got it. I'll tell him to fuck off, too. But I'm sure after I hang up, they're going to come back to see for themselves. You can come hang out with Landon and me for a while until they back off if you want."

Leigh's declaration makes me snicker, as she doesn't usually use that language. I lean in and hug her.

"If you don't mind."

"Not one bit." Leigh entwines her arm in mine and hurries me into her apartment.

"Landon is napping, which is something you look like you could use. Why don't you go lie down for a while in the guest room? I'll handle this for now, but you know you're going to have to deal with it soon."

"I know, just not right now."

Exhausted, I collapse onto Leigh's bed in her guest room and fall asleep picturing Jarrod's handwriting. *Sorry.* As if that will ever be enough.

...

THE JOYFUL SOUNDS of a toddler playing wake me up. I stretch before putting on my shoes and attempting to straighten my hair with my hands. I open the guest room door at the same time the doorbell rings. Quickly, I shut the door all but a crack so that I can hear who is there, although the flutters in my chest confirm that I already know. Finn's husky voice invades the space. The guest room door is down a straight hallway, which gives me a clear view of a portion of the living room. Landon runs from one end of my view toward the door until I can no longer see him. Leigh and Finn are talking, but their words are muffled. I can't make out what they're saying. Suddenly, Finn comes into view and he's holding Landon as they move their conversation into the living room. Moving my feet slowly and as gently as I can further into the hallway, Finn's words become clear.

"She came in to tell me she was getting hitched. I was wishin' her well and telling her it was okay to move on. That I had found my place in this world with Daphne. I would never hurt her like that. Tell me where she is."

The room silences as I slowly enter from the hallway. Finn gently lowers Landon to the floor, never taking his eyes off of me, and walks in my direction until he's so close to me that I feel the heat from his body.

"So that wasn't one of your cheap women you talked about?" I whispered.

"You just left and didn't let me explain. I would've introduced you. I would have *liked* to introduce you."

Not able to think of something to say, I stand in front of Finn, his hands on either sides of my hips, right where I like them to be. His blue eyes tell me every word he says is true. Suddenly, Leigh clears her throat and, taking one look at her, she's silently telling me to forgive my man.

"I think we should get out of Leigh's hair." I say.

"Lead the way, Daffodil." Finn motions his hand in front of him.

"No." Landon pouts. "Finny stay."

Finn turns as he kneels down to Landon and looks him in the eyes.

"I'll come back another day to play. Okay, buddy?"

Landon sadly nods as Leigh comes and scoops him up. Then she playfully shoos us out of the door.

Once inside my apartment—and Herman has been greeted properly —Finn picks me up from the ground and steadies me on my feet. Then he doesn't let go.

"One thing you should know about me, loyalty runs in my veins. I'm one person you'll never have to worry about doin' you wrong. So if you see somethin' that doesn't look right, ask me. I'm sorry—"

The sound of hard skin-to-skin contact echoes in the room. Ringing invades my ears, and black pixilation takes over my vision. The inside of my palm stings, and a red outline of five fingers begin to appear on Finn's cheek. My eyes blink rapidly to rid the darkness and to try to piece together what just happened. Finn stands strong, motionless but confused.

"I...I...I didn't mean to...that word—" I stumble, the tears fresh in my eyes.

"What word?"

I retract, step around Finn, and sit on the couch, staring down at my hand that just smacked his face. The couch dips beside me as Finn sits down.

"That was the last thing my brother ever said to me." The sadness almost instantaneously fades and turns to anger. Not able to sit anymore, I walk to the window and look out. "I don't know why the fuck people say sorry anyway. Why does that word all of the sudden excuse what a person has done? I know Jarrod felt badly about leaving me. But that didn't stop him from doing it. Sorry is just the pussy way of making yourself feel better about making someone else feel terrible. I never want to hear that word again."

"Noted. Come sit back down." Finn pats the couch next to him.

Tears continue to gradually fall down my face. It's irritating that I couldn't get them to fall at all in the beginning and now I can't get them to stop.

Taking a deep, calming breath, I sit sideways on the couch facing Finn.

"I want to explain what you saw," he says.

"I heard you talking to Leigh. I know who she was. She's your ex right? You said she's getting married. Why did she need to tell you?"

His hand reaches up to his scruffy chin and rubs it back and forth before speaking.

"You really want to hear this?" he asks.

"Yes."

"Mel and I were together for five years. We had everything planned out. Our wedding, how many kids we wanted, what part of Boston we wanted to live in, our entire lives."

"So what happened?"

"It just fell apart. I think she wanted to be ready, but she wasn't. A week before our wedding, she handed me the ring I gave to her and told me she couldn't do it anymore. She just left."

"That's awful."

"No lie, it was a kick straight to the balls. It destroyed me. I've never been angry with her though. I was glad she told me the truth before we got married. She felt terrible that she couldn't be what I wanted."

"Jesus. I'm not sure I could have forgiven so easily," I say, crossing my arms.

"Sometimes, shit happens that completely changes the direction you face. She didn't do anything wrong. Wasn't her fault that she didn't love me. It just didn't work out."

"If you feel that way, why haven't you had a serious girlfriend since her?"

Finn's face squints. "How did you know that?"

"Kael."

"That jackass has one hell of a big mouth. I said I wasn't mad at her. I can't help how I feel though. I didn't want anybody. Until you," Finn declares as he reaches for my hand. "And I won't say that word again."

"Don't do anything that would require you to."

Finn nods, and we sit quietly for a few minutes. I stare at the way Finn's thumb rubs the side of my hand so gently. Suddenly, his movement stills.

"Leigh said you went to the pub because you were upset. Why were you upset? She wouldn't tell me."

"I don't want to talk about it right now."

Finn nods and places his warm wet lips to mine. Our kiss halts as a loud knock comes from my front door. Finn grunts as I get up and open the door to find Ryan standing there.

"Ryan?" My hip cocks to the side. I place my hand on it to emphasize how utterly irritated I am with his sudden and constant presence.

"I had to see for myself that you're good. I'm staying in a hotel a few blocks down. Ally is coming to town tonight, and I wanted to see if you and Finn wanted to join us for dinner."

"Let me talk to Finn. I'm not sure if we're up for it tonight."

"I made reservations at Amadeo's Steakhouse for four, but if you can't make it, it's okay. Benson recommended the restaurant," he said. It irritates me that he even talked to Benson. But I supposed the blame is on me for that since they were all out looking for me last night.

"Can I call you in an hour and let you know?"

"Sure." Ryan leans in and wraps his arms around me. My body stiffens at the feel of his touch. Ryan has never hugged me before. "I'm glad you're okay. There's no way I could lose you both." Finally snapping out of it, I reciprocate his embrace, even though it feels awkward.

Finn pulls me gently out of Ryan's arms and into his side. "We'll come to dinner, see you later," Finn says.

Ryan tips his head at both of us, then leaves the doorway. Finn shuts and locks it. Turning to me, he reaches out for my hand and pulls me into the bedroom.

"I'm tired. Nap?" he asks.

A nap sounds amazing right now. The one I took at Leigh's house was interrupted perpetually by bad dreams. Finn rips his shirt over his head with one hand. He reaches to his side and pulls his handgun from his belt and places it on the nightstand by the bed. It's no secret in the bar that Finn carries a gun most of the time. But I've never seen it until now. Something about his fluid movements—and the way his eyes never leave mine as he undoes his pants and steps out of them—sends a slow burn through me. Instead of crawling into the bed, he walks to me in his boxers, grabs the hem of my shirt, and pulls it over my head. The instant the fabric leaves my skin his mouth comes close to mine but doesn't touch.

"I would never hurt you," he whispers. My body begs to feel his skin against mine, so I move forward, closing the extra space that was between us. Strong thick arms wrap around me as his lips touch mine. He gently pushes me back as his hands dip into my hair and his kiss deepens. The mattress presses against the back of my knees, and he lowers me onto it. His fingers pull on my waistband and he removes everything below my bellybutton. The slickness of his tongue glides up my leg and kisses the tender skin inside of my thigh before making his way up my body. Finn's touch frees me of sadness. It clears my head, and all I see is us.

"You scared me today," Finn whispers in my ear before he nibbles on it. "I thought you were gone. Please. Don't do that to me."

"Never again," I assure him.

As my body is worshiped by the man who loves every inch of me, I know I'll never doubt Finnegan O'Reilly again.

After Finn comes back from cleaning himself up in the bathroom, I hop up to go in next. Making my trip to the bathroom quick, I race back out to get into bed so that I can hear the sound of Finn's beating heart. But as I get closer to him, the feeling in the room is different than when I left it. Finn is sitting up in the bed and my nightstand light is on. He's reading something. I feel like I've swallowed my tongue, my heart pulses, and sweat collects in my palms. I run to Finn and rip Jarrod's letter out of his hands.

"That's what you were upset about."

"I never said that you could read that," I snip, angrier that the letter exists than I am that he read it.

"That ain't right. No wonder you took off last night. You've been taking in so much bullshit. Maybe you should talk to someone?"

"I've been talking to people all my life. You have no idea the amount of different doctors and psychiatrists I've been to with my brother. The absolute last thing I need to do right now is to go to them and say he's dead."

Carefully, I fold up the painful letter and place it back into the envelope. I put it in my dresser drawer. Later, when things aren't so raw, I'll decide what to do with it. Passing by the window on the way back to the bed, I happen to glance outside and see a rainbow against the darkened sky as the sun peeks out from the other side of my building. This particular rainbow has the brightest green I've ever seen. It's beautiful. Finn's body warms my back, as he wraps his arms around me and places a sweet kiss on my temple.

"You're going to be all right. I'll make sure to that. Let's just agree not to shut each other out. You don't want to talk to anyone else, fine. Talk to me. I'll listen."

I nod my head and hold onto his arms as we both watch the rainbow slowly fade into the sky. My stomach growls, and I glance at the clock.

"Looks like we need to get going if we're meeting Ryan for dinner. I'm going to run to my place to get something decent to wear. I'll send you a text when I'm downstairs."

"Why did you agree so fast to dinner with Ryan and his girlfriend? I thought you weren't a fan of his."

"I'm not, but I'd like to see how he acts with his girl around. Figure it'll do one of two things. I'll like him enough to tolerate him, or I'll never take my eyes off of him around you."

"I'm telling you, he's harmless. Just a spoiled childhood that caused a big ego."

Finn grunts and drops his hands from around me as he moves to gather his clothes. Just before he walks out of the room, he flashes me that side dimple that makes me want to cancel dinner and repeat what just happened on my bed.

"Get ready, Daffodil," Finn shouts from the living room right before I hear the front door shut and lock.

Reluctantly, I move from the window and head into my closet. I try on at least six outfits, but nothing seems nice enough for Amadeo's. I hate dressing up. Finally, I settle on a little black halter dress. It's casual, but you can dress it up a bit with some heels. Of course, I can't have plain heels with no flare, so I go for my pumps that lace up my legs. I spend a short time messily curling my long hair and backcombing a bit. Just as I finish the last swipe of bright red lipstick to my bottom lip, my phone chirps. I grab my purse and race downstairs. Finn is parked in a fire zone right in front of the building. As I open the door to his Wrangler, his face is solid. As I get in, Finn still hasn't stopped staring at me. A horn blares from behind us.

"What the hell is your problem?" I begin to look myself over thinking that I've spilled something or that I have something stuck to me.

Finn doesn't say a word but reaches for my hand and places it in his lap. Feeling the stiffness inside of his dark jeans, I can't help but start to laugh.

"First time I see you dressed like that, and now what the fuck am I supposed to do with this?"

"Well, we're in the middle of the street, and we have to be there in ten minutes when we're twenty away, so I would suggest getting yourself under control and start to drive." My laughter doesn't subside as he growls and adjusts himself.

The movements of the city out of the window slowly turn into a blur as my eyes lock into a daze. My mind takes me back to the last time I saw Jarrod, as it tends to do when I'm not doing something. The deep pain reverberates against the walls in my chest. Thankfully, I'm brought back into the current moment by the sudden warmth that takes over my hand. Finn looks at me with concern to which I grab onto his hand and force a grin. I tighten my hand around his, and he squeezes it once then doesn't let go the rest of the car ride to Amadeo's.

Walking into Amadeo's, I immediately spot Ryan sitting in a booth. As we get closer to him, Ally becomes visible in a gorgeous light blue oversized blouse dress. It's stunning against her tan skin. Her hair is neatly up in a ballerina bun, exposing large diamond drop earrings. She's perfectly put together, just like Ryan. The two of them look like they stepped out of a magazine advertisement. Any preconceived notions I had walking in here about the type of person Ally might be, disappear as her friendly smile and demeanor greet me. Her hand reaches out warmly and I grip it, returning her smile.

"It's nice to meet you, Ally."

"Yes. I'm so glad I'm able to finally put a face to all the stories."

Ally and I scoot all the way into the booth so the guys can sit on the ends. I'm anxious to learn more about her and how she ended up with Ryan.

Finn leans into the booth, placing a kiss on my cheek. "We'll be right back," he says, then he and Ryan walk up to the fancy bar that sits on the other side of the restaurant. Turning back to Ally, she looks just as confused as I do.

"As long as they aren't punching each other, I guess we don't need to worry," I say, shrugging.

Ally giggle uncomfortably, then her tone changes. "Listen, I'm so sorry about your brother."

Immediate disgust begins to churn in my stomach at that useless term. I swallow hard and calm myself quickly, as I can't lose it every time someone says it or brings him up.

"Thanks," I say curtly and take a long drink of water, trying to drown my internal rage.

"Ryan has been having a hard time."

It's obvious that Ryan is having a hard time just from his weird phone calls and suddenly showing up on my doorstep. But I wonder if there's more that I don't know.

"You mean he's just been sad a lot?" I ask, trying to see if she'll give me more.

"He disappears. Once he went on a business trip and didn't tell me. I called him for two days, but he didn't answer until he was on his flight back home. Then he came to Boston and I didn't know he was here until he picked up my phone call and told me. It's weird because he's never mentioned Boston before. It made a little more sense when I found out you lived here."

Some days, I wish I could disappear. So I know how he feels and I'm actually a bit jealous that he can just take off like that. Finn has become a beacon in the water for me though. But that doesn't mean that I don't understand wanting to get away from everything and wallow in your sadness for a little while. Thankfully, the waiter comes and breaks the conversation.

"Can I get you something to drink?"

"Yes. I'll have a sparkling water please," I say.

The waiter nods and places a drink in front of Ally that she must have ordered before we arrived, then rushes off again.

"What is it that you do, Ally? Ryan has mentioned that you travel often with your job."

"I'm a destination wedding planner. It sounds like it should be fun, but it's actually kind of stressful. Most brides are a bit of a handful, and

I have to make sure that everything is as perfect as it can be. The night of the wedding is fun though."

"No way. I don't think that sounds fun at all. I'd probably have a hard time not punching one in the face the minute she became a snotty little brat. I get that it's their wedding and all, but you don't have to be a beast to everyone around you. I've seen those shows."

Ally's laugh is contagious, and before I know it, I'm laughing right along with her. Our conversation continues to be light and easygoing. I'm completely taken by surprise with how much I like her. The guys come back, and they look happy, too. Maybe this isn't as bad as I thought it was going to be.

We spend more than a few hours in the restaurant ordering drinks, telling jokes, and just having a good time.

Ryan turns to Ally. "I forgot to tell you that I'm stopping by the center in New York tomorrow, so I can drop off those things you wanted to donate."

"Oh good," Ally replies.

"What's the center?" I ask.

Ally proudly smiles. "Ryan volunteers at a mental health center in New York. He teaches classes on business to help people believe in themselves and that they can succeed just like anyone else." Then she snuggles close to his side, and he wraps his arm around her shoulder.

Right then, I see what I think Jarrod saw. I'm so glad that we had this dinner together. I have a new appreciation for Jarrod and Ally is so sweet. After exchanging phone numbers, Ally and I make plans to go out tomorrow night. Ryan leaves in the morning for New York and Ally isn't leaving until the next day.

Back in the Wrangler, Finn grabs my hand, pulls it up to his face, and kisses the back of it. Seems to be something he likes to do often. For the first time since the death of Jarrod, I feel happy. And I don't feel guilty for it. I don't think my smile fades once all the way back to my apartment. Finn parks, we get out, and as soon as our bodies meet at the back of his Wrangler, he grabs my waist and his lips find their way to mine. His hands caress my skin, and my favorite feature appears on the side of his face, accompanied by a sly smirk.

"What are you thinking about, Finnegan O'Reilly?"

"How beautiful you look happy. I didn't realize it until tonight, but it's the first time I've seen you this way. I'm makin' it my mission to keep you lookin' just like this."

He grabs my hand and begins walking faster than usual.

"Why are we walking so fast?"

"I've had to control myself all night. I'm done with that shit."

CHAPTER NINE

MY DRESS IS STILL CRUMPLED on the floor from when Finn ripped it over my head and tossed it last night. I yawn and walk to the kitchen to get a cup of tea. My favorite mug is sitting on the counter waiting and underneath it is a note.

-Daffodil-

I tried to tell you goodbye this morning, but I'm not sure you were fully awake. I have to work today, and Kael wants tonight off. I owe him. I'll be late, so I'll see you tomorrow. If you need me, call.

-F-

As I'M WAITING for my tea to steep, my phone rings.

"Hey, Ally," I greet into the phone.

"Good morning. I was looking to do some shopping. Care to join me?"

"Sure. I just got up though, so I need to shower. You want to come to my house until I'm ready?"

"Yeah, that sounds great."

I give Ally my address and directions to get to my apartment. Shortly after I get out of the shower, I hear the buzzer from downstairs. Stopping myself from buzzing her right up, I press the talk button.

"Ally?" I ask.

"Hi, Daphne," she responds. I buzz her up and open the apartment door a crack as I race around my apartment trying to finish getting ready. Within a minute, Ally slowly opens the door and I wave for her to come in. She looks beautiful in her dark denim jeggings with a simple black blouse under a white blazer. The thought of shopping in high heels has never crossed my mind, but apparently, it's the way Ally rolls.

"This place is so cozy," she says, setting down her Louis Vuitton purse that's the size of a duffle bag. She slowly walks around, taking in the kitchen and living space. She walks to the window and smiles kindly. "This is a great view of the city."

"I love it here," I tell her. "You ready?"

She nods, picks up her bag with a perfectly white smile, and we head out for the day.

I'm exhausted after three stores. Ally is one hell of a star shopper. She spends forever in each one, looking down every aisle, then starting back at the beginning and going through it all again. We finally make it to a home store, which is more exciting to me since I buy most of my clothes online. Ally heads in first, and just before I completely enter the store, something in my peripheral vision grabs my attention. I turn to look and see nothing, but I stand there staring.

"You okay?" Ally asks, coming back out of the store to see why I didn't come in.

"I thought I just saw Ryan."

"No, he's in New York and won't be back until the day after tomorrow. You probably just saw someone who looks like him." She laughs, grabs my elbow, and leads me into the store. But I can't help but shake the feeling of being watched.

* * *

HOURS LATER, shopping has forced me to put my aching feet up at my apartment. Ally, on the other hand, is still shopping. And she's damn good at it, too. Looking around my apartment, I plan on where to put all the new items I bought that will be delivered tomorrow. I found the perfect side tables to my sectional and a few pillows. Ally found some beautiful crystal candlesticks. She said brides are always looking for pretty things to incorporate into their wedding, and it makes it easier for them if they like something that she already has. Even just the thought of weddings freaks me out. I never thought about marriage. One thing I do know is if the time should ever happen, I'm not going looking for crystal candlesticks.

I decide to use my time wisely and take a nap. Kicking off my Chucks, I flop myself onto the bed and close my eyes. Not five minutes into my peaceful quiet, I hear three knocks then a pause, followed by two knocks.

"Leigh," I yell in a zombie voice. Leigh comes walking in and flings herself onto my bed next to me. Herman quickly leaves my side and snuggles into Leigh's belly. "Traitor," I snip at him and Leigh laughs.

"I take it you and Finny Finn Finn made up," she teases.

"I will punch you in the face if you call him that again," I laugh. "I just jumped to conclusions. My head has been all foggy anyways and that just sent me over the edge. We're fine."

"I'm glad. He's good for you."

"How do you know that?" I ask.

"Vibes. You know I get vibes with people. That and he called me the other day."

"Oh?" My curiosity immediately peaks, and I sit up on an elbow.

"He said he wanted to talk to Landon about that promise he made to him about coming back to play." The smile that spread across her face is part wicked and part melty. I can't even pretend it doesn't make me melty, too. "Don't you dare let that man go."

"It's not in my plans."

Knowing that Leigh isn't going to let me sleep, I get up from the bed and walk into the kitchen to get a bottle of water. Leigh follows me.

"What are you doing tonight? Want to come over, order pizza, and watch something funny?"

"Love to, but I can't. I'm going out with Ally, Ryan's girlfriend tonight. Ryan is in New York for business and Ally doesn't leave until tomorrow morning. Do you want to come with? I think you would really like her."

"I can't. Carter is working tonight. Promise me you won't drink too much. It really freaked me out the other night."

"I won't. I think last time it was just too much with all the emotions running through me. I'll be fine."

Leigh shoots me a stern look and gives me a quick hug before she turns and walks out of my apartment.

I eat a quick dinner of leftover pizza and then put on dark wash jeans with a white V-neck T-shirt paired with black strappy heels and my favorite worn-in black leather jacket. My hair is in its signature bouffant, sleek on the sides but down in the back. I say goodbye to Herman on my way out. I text Ally to let her know that I'm on my way but I only make it halfway through typing when a voice shoots straight through me, stopping me from descending the last two steps of the buildings front stoop.

"Daphne."

"Mom?"

I race to stand in front of her. "Is Daddy okay?"

"Heavens, yes. He's fine."

Though her voice is annoyed, her hands grip tighter to her purse. Almost like she's nervous. My mother has never once come to Boston for a visit. Whatever she's here for must be important. Her driver, Tony, is standing next to her town car as if he's waiting for her to get back in.

"Do you want to come up?" I ask, turning to head back into the building.

"No," she says abruptly.

My body slowly turns back around. As if I should have expected anything different. Her long haggard face almost doesn't match her brown hair in a perfect chignon and her tailored crisp white dress suit.

"What are you doing here, Mom?"

She takes a long drawn in breath, then reaches into her purse and pulls out a blue envelope. My body stiffens. I've had enough of envelopes, letters and bad news to last a lifetime.

"If that's from Jarrod, I'm done. I can't take anymore. So if that's why you had Tony drive all the way here, it was a waste of your time."

I take three steps away from her intending on walking away and meeting Ally without any more conversation between us.

"Stop," she demands. I listen, but don't turn to face her. Maybe that will make whatever it is that she has to say bounce off of my back instead of sink right into my chest. "Jarrod wanted you to have what is left of his money from Gram. This is a copy of his will so you can see for yourself. You'll have to meet with the lawyer to sign some paperwork."

It doesn't surprise me that Jarrod left the rest of that money to me. It's not like I need it or want it, but it was from Gram. He knew how much I loved her. I would much rather have him here though, to spend it like an idiot like he usually did.

"Why didn't you just call me instead of driving all the way here to make me feel like the hated child I have always been?"

My mother blinks hard and visibly swallows. "I do not hate you, Daphne. I do not."

"Then why did you say—?"

"I don't have time for this, Daphne."

"If you aren't wanting to talk to me or spend time with me, then why are you here?"

"Jarrod wrote me a letter. In it, he told me to come here and see where you live. He wanted me to tell you about the money in person. Now I've done what he asked of me."

I stand dumbfounded as she turns and Tony opens the door for her. Before getting in, she quietly speaks over her shoulder. "I love you." She swiftly gets in the car. As the taillights disappear into the sea of cars on the Boston street, I can't help but notice her voice sounded different. Once I pull myself out of the stupor my mother left me in, I look down at the blue envelope that contains Jarrod's will. I toss it into my purse and slowly walk toward the bar. I have no intention of ever actually reading it.

Walking into Zuco's, I hear Ally yell my name from a side table. I nod to her and hold up one finger as I head to the bar.

"What can I get ya?" the bartender asks.

"Jameson, make it a double, and an Irish Redhead." I spit out.

"Got ya' covered."

Two seconds later, I down the double shot of Jameson, then take the Irish Redhead to the table to join Ally.

"Hey, is everything all right?" she asks, looking over my face.

"I just had an unexpected run-in. I'm a little frazzled, but I'm fine."

Ally's eyes scan the bar and she jumps in her seat excitedly.

"You want to play darts?" She points to the empty corner where they have the darts set up on the wall.

"Sure."

Ally and I grab our things, and we walk to the back corner, taking over the bar height table that's closest to the dartboard. Ally takes the darts out of the board and hands me the red ones. After a few rounds, two guys appear at our table that we are leaning against, but Ally chases them off so fast I could barely get a word in.

"Oh, Finn's going to like you," I snicker.

After four games of darts and a few rounds of drinks, we are laughing like teenagers.

"You missed," I snort. Ally's dart is stuck in the wall next to the dartboard. When we first arrived, she was hitting the bullseye.

"Shut up," she squeals as she yanks it out of the wall. "You aren't any better."

We laugh harder as my dart falls so short of the board it falls to the ground. The night helps me forget about my mother's coldness. Unfortunately, that doesn't continue on the walk home. All I can think about is that never-ending look of disappointment in her eyes. The forced declaration of love because that is what is expected in her world. Before I sink lower into the depths of my internal troubles, my phones rings, and I rush for it.

"Finn." I greet, a little too excitedly.

"Hey, Daffodil. Are you home?"

"Walking there now. Where are you?"

"I'm about to leave the pub. I'm on my way to you."

"Okey dokey."

There is silence on the other end for a minute.

"Where are you?"

"A block from my house, why?"

"You're slurring your words. You should have taken a cab. I'll meet you there."

I shrug and place my phone back in my bag, and I hightail it to my building. Reaching my apartment, I don't see Finn anywhere so I sit on my stoop to wait for him. I remember watching a streetlight change from red to green and then nothing else until someone touches me. A small scream comes out as arms wrap around my body, lifting me.

"I've got you, Daffodil."

Finn carries me all the way up into my apartment. He places me gently on the couch, then sits next to me.

"Why do you smell like beer?"

"I got too close to Tasha and her tray." His answer is abrupt and angry.

"Are you mad at me?"

"You're damn right I am. You wanna explain to me how you think it's okay to pass out on your stoop?"

"I was waiting for you. I wanted to see you all night. I thought you said you weren't coming over."

Finn breathes in heavily though his nose as he angles himself back onto the couch. I place my head in my hand and suddenly can't seem to stay awake.

"I wanted to talk to you about something, but it will have to wait until the morning."

Finn helps me stand and the warmth of his hand spreads across the small of my back as we head to the bedroom. I strip my clothes and pull on an oversized ripped up t-shirt. The shower turns on as I crawl into bed. I try to stay awake until Finn comes to bed but the exhaustion wins.

* * *

As my eyes open and adjust to the light, a broad-shouldered man lying on his back next to me grabs my attention. His head is cocked to one side, eyes closed. I can't help but to study every line of his face, even though my favorite one is hidden. My peaceful admiration of Finn next to me is cut short by my fucking ringing phone. Glancing at the clock, I'm even more irritated that it's nine in the morning. Ryan just can't get this through his damn head.

"Hello," I say in an annoyed whisper.

"Hey. Ally said you two drank a bunch last night. I just wanted to make sure you got home okay."

"Ryan. I'm fine and stop—"

I get cut off by Finn taking the phone out of my hand.

"Ryan." His tone is clearly not playing. "Good." Then he hangs up and puts the phone on the nightstand next to him. He snuggles back into the blankets. I stay up on an elbow, confused about the conversation that just happened between Finn and Ryan.

"What was that?"

"What?" Finn asks, knowing damn well what I'm referring to. He sits up on an elbow too so we are face to face. "I need to talk to you about something."

"Okay. You're scaring me a little."

"My parents are coming in tomorrow. They'll be here for a week and a half, and they'll be staying at my condo."

"That will be really nice for you and Kael to have them around. I'm sure you miss them."

Selfishly, my insides begin to shudder at the thought of Finn being busy with his family for an entire week. With Finn gone, there's nothing to focus on other than my solitude.

"Do you need me to pick up some extra work at the pub or something so you can spend more time with them while they're here?"

"No. I want you to be with me while I'm with them," he says gently. I swallow the lump that's developed in my throat. "If you want to. Do you want to?"

"I'm on the schedule the rest of this week. I...I..."

"I want you to meet my family. My mother is especially wanting to meet you."

My eyes dart to the floor. I hadn't even bothered mentioning Finn to my mother or my mother to Finn. What would I even tell him? A darkness settles over me as it usually does when I think of all the disappointment I've been to my mother.

"What if she hates me?"

I despise the fact that I actually care about what others might think. I put on this façade that what people say and do don't bother me. I've spent most of my life pretending like my feelings don't get hurt and my glass walls are made of steel. So, I protect myself by grabbing onto the few people I trust, like Leigh, and holding onto them tight. Everyone else, I try extremely hard to avoid.

"You don't have to worry about that."

"I'm not like normal people. It's not easy to—"

Finn grabs my chin and forces my eyes to meet his blues. "I said, don't worry about it. A little trust and a week, that's all I'm askin'."

The pit in my stomach only grows, but how can I say no? "Okay," I whisper. "Shit."

"What now?" Finn asks.

"I need to go shopping. Get some nicer clothes."

"No way. You wear what you usually do. I love you how you are. Don't go changin' for anyone."

Heat rises in my cheeks as I lean into the man I love. My lips press against his, slow and deep.

"I hate to leave, but I have to go to the pub and get everything in line so that the week goes smoothly. Regan is on the schedule for most of the time my parents are in. When they leave, I'll be slammed at the pub and might need you to help if you can. I'll see you tonight when you come in for your shift."

He bends and kisses me again, and his dimple appears just as he walks out of the bedroom. The anxiety rushing through me is painful. I know how important Finn's family is to him. If his mother doesn't like me just like my own doesn't, it would be the end of us. The end of hope.

CHAPTER TEN

"STOP FIDGETING," Finn says. "Not a muscle in your body has been still for the last six hours."

He's right. I'm exhausted and feel like a complete mess. It's getting worse the closer we get to the baggage claim area to meet his parents.

"I'm going to the bathroom. I'll be right back."

He nods and I race off to the ladies room.

Once in front of the mirror, I take a deep breath, reach into my purse, and grab my hair brush. Meeting Finn's family is an entirely foreign experience. I've never met anyone else's parents before. I'm desperate to make a good impression. Removing my messy bun, I brush my long hair and French braid it neatly down the center of my head. My shaky hands apply the nude lip gloss that I borrowed from Leigh, and I straighten my new black flowy top.

Looking into to the mirror, I stare at a different version of myself. It's not just the makeup or the hair or the covered-up tattoos. It's like looking at a young version of my mother. My gram was a different lady to my brother and me than she was with my mother. It was obvious when the two were together that they weren't close. I wonder if my mother ever looked at herself in the mirror and felt this way. Without warning, tears form along the bottom of my eyes. I'm sure she didn't want to be treated the way I am. Made to feel the way I've been made to feel. I've never felt good enough. Worthy enough. Always the different one. Always out of place, no matter where I might be standing.

My head dips as a tear rolls down my nose, and I watch it fall to the ground. Then I notice something barely sticking out the small pocket on the side of my purse—the pocket that I never use—but the zipper is open, and there's something that catches my eye. I reach in and find a slightly smashed bright yellow daffodil. Looking at the damaged petals, a replica of how I feel, I'm reminded of how I got to this point. I swore to never let anyone change the person I am inside. Even if that meant more pain than peace. Quickly grabbing a makeup remover wipe from my purse, I wipe off the horrible nude gloss and replace it with my deep red matte lipstick. The perfect braid is taken out, and I replace it with a loose side braid that's messy but still looks done. My sleeve of tattoos is only partially hidden by the cold shoulder, flowy black shirt that I actually like.

Returning to Finn, still nervous but a little braver than when I went into the bathroom, I grab his face and plant a kiss on his lips. I laugh as I forgot that I just applied the red lipstick.

"What was that for? And why are you laughin' so— damn."

Finn's eyes travel from my head to my mouth. I grab a wipe from my purse and clean the lipstick from his lips.

"Whatever happened in that bathroom, I like it."

"Funny thing, I found this in my purse." I hold up the daffodil smiling at him.

"I didn't put that in there," he says, confused.

"If you didn't put it in my purse, then how did it get there? Leigh," I say smiling.

As Finn and I look at each other, people begin to file into the baggage claim area.

"Holy shit. Do you think this is all going too fast?"

A laugh comes from deep within Finn. "I've been waiting for you to be mine for two years, so no, I don't."

Through the rush of people, Finn spots his parents and points to them. The first thing I notice is his mother's deep red hair. It's short, spunky, and a much deeper red than the normal redhead. Her smile lights up her face as they walk in our direction. I've seen them at the pub before. They came into town once to run the pub when Finn was in the hospital. But I was leaving to Jarrod's house as they came in so I never got the chance to formally meet them. Finn releases my hand as his arms stretch out for his mother.

"I'm so glad to see you, Finnegan," she says, now fully in his embrace.

"Hi there, I'm Eoin." Finn's dad reaches his arm out and shakes my hand. As he smirks at me, it becomes obvious where Finn's dimple came from.

"Daphne," I reply, matching his kind smile.

"I've heard so much about you," he says before Finn's mom throws her arms around me.

Eoin moves to his son and embraces him as all the breath in my body is being squeezed out of me.

"Mom. Let go," Finn says, chuckling and pulling gently on my elbow to free me.

"Siobhan," Finn's mom says as she places her hand over her chest. "I'm so happy to meet you." Her wide smile causes her eyes to squint. Immediately, I feel the warmth and authenticity radiating from her. So different from the parents I've known.

"C'mon," Finn says, grabbing the suitcase from out of his mother's hand. "Let's get you guys settled."

I sit quietly in the backseat against Finn's wishes. I can sit next to him whenever I want to, but his mother can't. Siobhan talks the entire drive to Finn's condo. I've never seen the inside of Finn's condo. There's no real reason why; we've just never had to go there. Since Kael lives here too, it's just easier for Finn to come to my place.

Finn opens the door to his home and motions his parents to walk in. As I approach Finn, he pulls me into him and plants a kiss on my lips. The smell of lemon wafts through the space. It's a beautiful condo with dark hardwood floors, clean lines, and an open floor plan. It's much bigger than my apartment.

"Where should we put our things, Finnegan?" Eoin asks.

"My bedroom. You guys are going to be sleeping in there while you're here."

"Where are you sleeping?"

"I'll probably just crash on the couch."

"You're going to sleep on the couch for a week and a half?" Siobhan turns to Eoin. "I told you we should have gotten a hotel room."

"You can come stay with me," I blurt out, facing Finn. I shut my mouth quickly, but obviously it's too late. I've just invited Finn to basically move in with me for the next week and half, in front of his parents no less. Not knowing them or how they would react to Finn sleeping at my house, I should have talked to him about this privately. I stare at the floor, not wanting to make eye contact in fear of seeing a familiar disappointed look. I could crawl into a hole.

Finn puts his arm around my waist. "Might not be a bad idea. If it's okay with you. That way, my parents and Kael can stay here, and everyone will have a bit of space. Is that okay with you guys?" Finn asks, pointing to his parents.

"As long as that's what you both want. I feel wrong for pushing you out of your own home."

Siobhan's voice didn't seem displeased, so I take a chance and look up to see her friendly smiling face. My foot should stay planted firmly on the ground and not in my mouth, so instead of saying anything, I smile and nod.

"Good, that's settled. I'll stay at Daphne's, and you guys can have your run of the place." Finn looks at me with a devilish grin.

Siobhan yawns and Eoin plops himself down on Finn's crisp black leather sofa.

"Why don't you two rest for a little while and we'll come back around dinner?"

"That sounds great. I think I might take a nap." Siobhan says. "I don't care what we do for dinner, so you two plan something. We aren't picky."

Finn makes sure that his parents have everything they need before we leave. As we walk to Finn's Wrangler, his perfect dimpled smirk comes out, and I just know something devious is about to come out of his mouth.

"Are you going to clear a spot in your dresser or closet for me?"

"I suppose my concert shirts can go in the same drawer as my bar shirts," I chuckle, handing him the spare key to my apartment I keep in my purse.

"Oh, this week is going to be fun," he says, pushing it onto his key ring. "You okay with goin' to the pub real quick so I can update Kael on what's going on and check on things?"

"Of course."

Walking through the pub, I become acutely aware of a few heads turning. Tasha smiles and nods at me. As Finn gives my hand a slight squeeze, I realize that we have just made a statement in the pub. Our relationship hasn't been a secret, but we also haven't been flaunting it or openly telling people about it. Instead of it freaking me out like I thought it would, I confidently hold onto his hand and love every minute.

Finn opens the office door and I'm taken aback. Ally is sitting across the desk from Kael.

"Ally? What are you doing here?" I question her confused. Last I knew, Ally was back in Albany.

"I had a meeting in town with a new client and thought I would swing by the pub. I wanted to grab you up and have a night on the town. But I didn't know family was coming in. Next time." Ally smiles and stands from the chair. "Kael, thanks for the chat."

"You bet," he answers.

After Ally leaves the room, I sit in the chair across from Kael and text Leigh to warn her about Finn staying with me for a while.

"So there's been a little change in plans." Finn tells Kael. "Mom and Dad are going to stay in the condo with you, and I'm going to spend the nights at Daphne's while they're in town."

"Great." Kael's brusque response catches my attention, but Finn doesn't seem to notice.

"I have to grab a few things from the storeroom. I'll be right back,"

Finn says as he exits the office, leaving the two of us alone. I've never felt nervous or uncomfortable around Kael and we've spent a lot of time together here at the pub. But right now, sitting here, I've never felt more anxious.

"Why are you looking at me like that?"

"I tried to warn you," he says, shaking his head.

"Warn me? What the hell are you talking about?"

"I told you he was going to fall fast and hard. Now here you are, meeting our parents. For fuck's sake you have him practically moving in."

"So what? Why does it bother you that Finn and I are together? Do you not like me or something?"

"Daphne, I like you a lot. But I've watched you give Finn false hope. I've watched you hurt him, twice already. I know what you did in this office. I also know that afterwards, you brushed him off and then disappeared for long periods of time. He's been fighting his feelings for you since you walked into this pub. As much as I like you, I'll always love my brother more. All I'm saying is if you aren't in it with everything you've got, end it now."

"I would never intentionally—" Finn coming back into the room makes me shut my mouth quickly. I don't want him to know what Kael and I were talking about.

"Did you work it out with Regan so that you can have dinner with us tonight?" Finn asks Kael.

"Yep, I'll be there."

"Great. We're going to head to Daphne's for a little while. Mom and Dad are resting for a bit. We'll see you later."

Kael nods as he watches Finn grab my hand and walk out of the room.

* * *

Right as I snuggle into the side of Finn on my couch, my phone rings. One look at the screen and I close my eyes, tilt my head back, and give a little groan.

"Don't answer it if you don't want to."

"I'll wonder if something is wrong if I don't," I tell him as I hit the green button and answer the phone.

"Hi, Ryan."

"Hey. I want to sit down and talk to you about the house, but I don't want to do it over the phone. Can I come over tomorrow?"

"I can't tomorrow. Finn's parents are in town for the next couple of days, and if I'm not working at the pub, I'll probably be busy. Maybe Monday?"

The thought of having this conversation with Ryan makes me want to cry. I don't want to be planning how to get rid of my brother's house. I want him there, living in it. Lately, it's been easy to get lost in Finn and our life that we're living right now together. But times like this bring the real world crashing right back down on me.

"Yeah, Monday will work." Ryan's voice sounds just as depressed as I feel.

"Is that all you needed?"

"Yep. I'll talk to you later, Daphs."

The phone disconnects, and I feel the burn in the tip of my nose. The type of feeling I get before tears form in my eyes. I breathe in deeply, trying to will the feeling away so that I don't break down again.

"You want some tea?" I ask Finn as I head into the kitchen.

"No thanks." He joins me and pulls me away from the counter so that our faces are close. "You okay? What did Ryan say to make you upset?" His lips are straight and tight together. I know he wants any reason to be mad at Ryan.

"We have to talk about Jarrod's house, so he's coming to Boston next week so that we can do that."

Finn takes a deep breath, places a quick soft kiss on my nose, and reaches into the cupboard to grab my favorite mug. He opens my tea bag and places it into the mug. Then he moves to my kettle and turns it on to heat the water. While we're waiting for the high-pitched signal of the water boiling, the palms of his hands rest softly on my hips.

"It's not gonna be easy. If you need me, I'm there. Just say the word and I'll be right at your side."

My head falls into his firm chest, and he kisses the top of my head, leaving his lips lingering as he wraps his arms around me. Lifting my eyes up to his and going up on my tiptoes, I press my lips against his. My mouth opens, and he takes the invitation, caressing my tongue with his. Wanting to feel more of him, my fingertips move themselves up the sides of his shirt and to the bulk of his shoulders. Finn's grip on me tightens as my hands continue their voyage, moving faster and firmer across his body. The heat builds as our breath quickens, and Finn's mouth moves from my mouth to the side of my neck. His body pushes me slowly back against the counter, and he reaches under my knee to pull it up so that he can nestle his body between me. His other hand gently pushes the spaghetti strap of my dark gray shorts romper off of my shoulder. I tilt my head to the side as his wet lips reappear on my clavicle, and his fingertips continue to expose more of my skin. My leg lowers as he moves his hand from under it to fully remove my clothing. I barely get my foot out of the romper when he grabs my waist and hoists me onto the island. Reaching up, he grips the back of my neck as his mouth closes around mine. The sound of a zipper coming undone about has *me* coming undone. I grab Finn's shirt and rip it off of him. The muscles of his forearm tense around my back as he lines himself up. I wrap my arms around his neck and graze my teeth along his jaw, causing him to hiss as he slips inside of me. My head throws back as he begins his rhythmic thrusts. As I lose the ability to hold onto him any longer, I lean back, lying flat across the island, and Finn's hand rests in between my breasts over my heart. The loud whistle of the kettle cuts through our moans as I get closer to peaking.

"Damn." Finn groans and I know he's there, and with the increased pace, so am I. Gripping his biceps, I cry out as the rush flows through me. Finn buries himself deep and his eyes become lazy.

"I guess we should clean the kitchen before we go," he snickers.

ARRIVING AT FINN'S CONDO, I'm still nervous but not as much as earlier when I met his parents for the first time. It's after seven and

Kael has been texting Finn for the last twenty minutes, telling him to hurry up and that he had picked up pizza, salad, and breadsticks on his way home from the pub. Walking into the door, I'm greeted with the same friendly smiles that I received at the airport. Siobhan immediately envelops me in her arms before she moves to her son. Eoin nods in my direction with a kind smile. But then there's Kael. He's already sitting at the table full of food, and he looks exceedingly annoyed.

"Let's eat. I'm sure it's already cold anyway since you two took your sweet time getting over here," Kael says.

"Now that's enough outta ya'. It'll be fine," Siobhan scolds him.

We all take seats, and of course, I end up between the two O'Reilly boys. I hate feeling like there's a problem between Kael and me.

Most of the dinner is quiet other than small talk. Some about the weather in Ireland and how great it is compared to Boston. Then Eoin starts talking about the pub and the atmosphere changes. You can actually feel the weight of the air increase.

"I think you two need to change your primary demographic. You're pullin' in all these young college kids when you should be focusin' more on pullin' in the older more prolific crowd."

"What we're doing is just fine, Dad," Finn spits.

"From what I've heard, you're on the border of not doing fine. You've got to straighten things out before they get out of control."

Finn shoots a cutting glare to Kael. I don't look to see what his reaction is because I feel as though I shouldn't even be here for this conversation.

"Dad. We're fine. We've got people in the pub constantly. Our inventory is good and controlled. I've even been toying with the idea of creating some merchandise to appease the customers."

"You have always done things arseways. You're trying to appeal to the wrong demographic. The older businessman isn't going to walk around with your sleeveless O'Reilly's shirt," Eoin says, chuckling.

"I've got people askin' the bartenders every day if we sell our shirts. It's a missed opportunity if we don't."

"Ha. That's another problem you've got goin' on."

"What's that?" Finn's voice is raised and his muscles are tense. Siobhan flashes me an embarrassed half smile.

"You need to focus on finding good employees—not ones who spill full trays of products or who disappear for weeks at a time, then suddenly show back up."

A brick hits me in the chest as I realize he's referring to me. I blink rapidly. After all, he's right. No other establishment would have put up with that.

Finn swallows hard and abruptly stands up, throwing his chair backwards. Siobhan and I jump at the loud crash of the chair hitting the floor. Finn places his hands on either side of his plate and leans over the table toward his dad. I chance a glimpse of Kael and he's looking at me as if I'm the one to blame. He shakes his head at me with disappointment. A look I've been trying to avoid from anyone. I'm pulled away from Kael's obvious disapproval of me by Finn yelling, "That is none of your God damned business."

"Eoin, that's enough," Siobhan says, looking angry. "What has gotten into all of ya'?"

There's no way I want to be part of this. Knowing what a burden I have been on Kael, Finn and the other staff at O'Reilly's these past years has always made me feel guilty. Slowly, I rise from the table and look to Eoin.

"I didn't mean to weigh down the pub. I never wanted to be a burden." I feel as though I should apologize, but there's no way I can make myself say that word. "I didn't mean to. Excuse me." I rush out of the room, and I hear Finn calling my name, but I'm not stopping. I run straight out of Finn's condo and out to the sidewalk.

"Stop. Daphne, stop."

"I just have a headache. I'm a bit overwhelmed, and I can't take all of this right now." My voice cracks. "I just can't."

Finn wraps his arms around me and places his lips briefly on my forehead. "Let me take you home. I'm about ready to get out of here myself."

"I'm okay, I promise. I'll take a cab; you should talk this out with him." My eyes angle to the pavement.

"He didn't realize he was talking about you. Kael just has a big ass mouth and tells them everything, but I know he didn't know it was you."

"What he said wasn't a lie." I shrug haphazardly. "I did that. Many times. I put your business and you in a tight spot. I'm a liability to have around. I don't want you fighting because of me. Please stay and work it out, I just want to go home and lie down."

"I'll be there as soon as I can," he says.

As I enter my dark apartment, I kneel to the ground when Herman comes running. This is the exact reason I love animals. There's no expectations, no conditions, just acceptance. After he begins to purr, I carry him through the darkness and set him on the end of my bed while I get ready and climb in, too. My body and mind exhausted, it doesn't take but a few minutes to fall asleep.

I awaken to the sound of my door opening. My heart lunges out of my chest for a minute before I hear Finn's voice say, "Hey there, buddy." Noticing that Herman isn't on my bed, I know he went to greet Finn. It doesn't take long before the bed dips beside me. He reaches over and places a kiss on my shoulder and his hand on my hip as he pulls me into his side.

"No one would see you as a liability. And if someone makes you feel that way, you tell me. I'll take care of them."

If only I could tell Finn that it's Kael making me feel this way. But I can't. I lay still until Finn's breath evens out. My eyes remain open because my brain won't shut off. Between Eoin and Kael's disapproval, maybe I need to step back.

CHAPTER ELEVEN

FINN TOOK off before I woke up. He left me a note saying that his parents were going to be visiting some friends tonight so he was going to work and he would see me there. I'm a little surprised since Finn said he was going to have Regan working most of this week. But I'm also looking forward to working.

As I walk in the pub, Tasha greets me with a squeal and a smile as usual. From her soaked pink blouse, I'd she's had another eventful day. She rushes around the bar, cashes out, and runs out of the pub. I take a quick scan of the pub but I don't see Finn or Kael, so I stick my purse in my usual place under the bar and get to work. Twenty minutes later, Kael, Finn, and a woman I've never seen before walk out of the office. Finn flashes me a full smile as the brothers continue talking behind the bar.

"Who were they talking to?" Danna, another waitress, asks as she comes up next to me.

"How should I know?"

"Well, you are the owner's girlfriend. I would guess that you would know if they're bringing in more waitresses or bartenders."

"Nope. He didn't tell me anything about it."

"Huh," she says, snotty, and then walks to one of her tables.

I try to keep my distance from Finn, but every time he gets within arm's reach of me, his hands make contact with my body. His touch makes my mind go fuzzy. As I'm looking for salt to fill the shakers, Finn comes up behind me. He wraps his massive arms around my shoulders and kisses my ear. For a split second, my head tilts to the side and my eyes close, wanting more. But I force my eyes back open, push out of his grip, and head back toward the bar.

A busy hour has passed since I last saw Finn. Kael is walking in my direction as I'm entering an order into the computer. *Great.*

"Finn wants to see you in the office," Kael spits out, a look of irritation on his face.

"I'll go as soon as my table leaves."

"No. He wants you in there now. I'm supposed to finish this for you."

Sighing loudly, I slam my order pad on the bar and stomp back to the office. I throw open the door and I'm stunned to see Eoin sitting in the chair across from Finn. My eyes wide and not sure what I'm walking into, I slowly shut the door behind me. Eoin walks to me, grabs my hands, and his familiar blue ocean eyes look into mine.

"Oh, Daphne. I'm so sorry. I had no idea."

Behind Eoin, I see Finn flinch at his father's use of my most hated word.

"It's okay. It was my fault I needed so much time off and the pub was shorthanded repeatedly. I probably should have just quit."

Eoin's head jolts back, and Finn sits further in his chair behind the desk.

"There's no way Finn would have let you go. See, my son here loves you, and since he owns this place, he makes the decisions. I overstepped last night. Please, forgive me."

"Of course," I say, letting my shoulders drop from their tensed position. Eoin moves forward, enveloping me in his arms.

"Thank goodness. I don't think this dry shite would ever speak to me again, had I rushed you off. I don't know how he managed to snag you, but he is a jammy bastard." Eoin chuckles as he nods to his son and exits the office.

Turning to Finn, I ask, "What's a jammy bastard?"

Finn's muscles contract as he pushes himself out of the chair. "It means I'm lucky." As the heat from his body gets close to me, I back away from him until my back hits the wall of the office. He places his hands on the wall on either side of me. "Something is up with you, Daffodil. You won't let me touch you. You barely look me in the eye. Tell me what's wrong. I'll fix it."

There's nothing I want more than to tell Finn that Kael has made me feel like I'm not good enough for him. But there's already obvious tension between the men in the O'Reilly family and I want nothing to do with being a part of any more.

"My mother came to Boston the other night and it's been bothering me. That's all," I lie.

"What? After she said those heinous things to you on the phone? What the fuck did she want?"

"I don't want to talk about it right now. I'm having a hard time being anywhere other than inside my own mind. Keeping busy helps, so I should probably get back to my tables."

"That's not it," he says, eyeing me closer. "I feel it. Tell me."

"I can't," I whisper, then push out of his arms and walk out of the office.

* * *

WAKING UP, I turn to the side and see that Finn didn't end up coming to bed last night. The apartment is quiet other than the meowing coming from Herman. Finn is gone, and after looking all over, he didn't leave a note. The blanket he used last night is folded neatly at the end of the couch, and there's a funny feeling in my stomach. Then I hear the knocks on the door. Rhythmic knocks tell me Leigh is about to walk in, so I continue my walk to the kitchen.

I smile at Leigh when she opens the door slightly and only sticks her head through.

"Am I interrupting anything?" Her grin is as wide as her face.

"No. Finn's not here." Balancing my bowl of cereal, I carefully make my way to the couch. Leigh busts through the door and plops down beside me. It only takes her a second before she picks up on my vibe.

"What's wrong?" she asks cautiously.

"Nothing can ever be easy."

"That doesn't tell me anything. Did Finn do something?"

A small snicker pops out of my chest. At this point, I'm not sure that man is capable of doing anything wrong.

"No."

"Stop talking in riddles and spill it," she says annoyed.

Holding up one finger, I continue to shove my sugar and cinnamon squares in by the spoonful. If she wants the whole story, she's going to have to wait until I'm done with my cereal. I will not eat soggy squares. I take my last bite and set what's left in my bowl on the ground. Herman happily laps up the tiny bit of milk.

"Kael. Kael is what's wrong right now."

"Finn's brother? I thought you two got along really well."

"Yes. We always have. Even now it's weird because I don't feel like he doesn't like me. He just doesn't want me with Finn. He's told me on a few occasions that he doesn't like us together and that I should leave now before I hurt him worse."

"What?" she snips.

"Part of me thinks he could be right. I've hurt him already. I don't deserve him."

"Stop saying you don't deserve him. You dedicated your entire life to another human being. You deserve more than the average person if you ask me."

"I just don't know what to do. I love him."

"Then stop letting others tell you how to live your life. The relationship that the two of you have is no one else's business. If Finn loves you, that's his decision. Kael has no say in the matter."

"I don't know, Leigh. Family is everything to Finn. If his family can't support us, I don't know what he'll do. I don't want to be responsible for that." I place my elbow on the armrest of the couch as

Herman's soft fur brushes against my skin. He purrs and mats the blanket I have over my lap.

"Have you told Finn?"

"I can't. If I tell him, it would cause a war for sure. Finn would be so angry."

"Well. That should tell you something right there," she says matter-of-factly.

Not wanting to talk about it anymore, I nod and turn on the TV. I don't want to lose Finn. But I know what it's like to not have a supportive family. I can't do that to him.

After watching a few shows of people buying islands and wishing I were one of them, Leigh heads home. Just as I start to head to the shower, my buzzer goes off. Remembering Finn's words, I resist just buzzing whoever it is up.

"Hello?" I ask into the speaker.

"Daphne dear? It's Siobhan. Can I come up?"

My eyes wide, my body stiffens. I slowly take a look around my messy apartment and panic.

"Daphne?"

"Oh, yes. Yes, come on up."

The second I let go of the TALK button, I fly into action. Picking up the blanket that ended up on the floor, the empty bowl that was still under my coffee table, and, not to mention, the papers and mess scattered all over my apartment, I'm completely out of breath when I hear a light tapping on my door. Before opening it, my eyes close. I inhale deeply though my nose and out my mouth. Then I calmly open the door, and I'm greeted by her kind squinty-eyed smile.

"Please, come in."

"I hope I'm not stepping out of place by coming here."

"Not at all. Would you like some tea? We could sit at the table."

"I would love some," she says.

Standing in the kitchen waiting on the tea kettle, I can see Siobhan in the other room looking around my tiny apartment. *What is she thinking looking around here?* I don't feel judged, but I also don't know how she is analyzing my place. The kettle beeps, and I quickly pour the boiling water into two mugs and place a black tea bag into each.

"Oh, thank you. Tea is so calming, don't you think?"

Nodding, I set down both of the cups onto the table, and then take a seat opposite of Siobhan. She takes a sip of her tea and gently places the cup back onto the table.

"Do you know why the rose bush has prickles?" My eyebrows furrow at the surprise of that question. I know nothing about flowers so I shake my head. "The rose is sweet and slightly fragile. The prickles protect the plant from being eaten by animals." She then picks up her cup and continues to take sips. I am completely confused at her statement. "Finnegan is a rose. He may not look like a rose. He looks like a beast walking, all hard and macho. But my Finnegan is sweet and fragile. Kael, well, he is the prickles. He is only trying to protect his brother."

She knows everything.

"I know he is," I say. "I want to sit down and talk to Kael, but every time I try, something interrupts us. I don't want to be responsible for the family fighting."

"Daphne, that's what families do. They argue, then they get over it and find something else to argue over. I wanted to come over and tell you to ignore Kael. Nothing he says matters to you or to Finnegan. My boy loves you, and if Kael doesn't settle down, I'm quickly going to become prickles."

Then she flashes me a devilish grin before going back to her tea. I copy her move and take a drink of mine too as I digest what she just said. Thankfully, she seems to be on my side. It calms me to know that Finn has told his mom how much he feels for me. I'm also surprised to realize how much I trust her.

"Sometimes I wonder if he is right. It's hard to think that I'm capable of loving when I still have so much sorrow."

I try to will away the tears that have formed in my eyes as I look to my lap so that Siobhan wouldn't notice. Once I think I've gotten myself cleared up, I glance in her direction to see she hasn't taken her eyes off of me.

"There is rarely love where tragedy hasn't treaded first. The ability to love to the greatest extent comes from the ability to feel pain so deep, you don't know how you lived through it."

Sitting together at my dining room table with Finn's mom giving me reassurance that I'm not a lost soul, peaks a bit of internal power I hadn't noticed before. It's the first time someone I respect gave me a pep talk. One that every word sank into me, forming this little ball of strength.

"Also, I want to apologize for my gobshite husband last night. You should know, he didn't know it was you and he has no idea about your brother. Finnegan told me, but I haven't breathed a word of that to another soul. It's not my story to tell. For the record, he would have been just as lenient with your position at the pub as Finnegan was if he knew."

"I just worry about causing a rift in your family. You all seem so close, and I know what it's like to have the opposite. I never want Finn to experience that."

"Nothing will tear this family apart. You don't have to worry about Finnegan feeling that way, and the day that you become an O'Reilly, you won't ever experience that feeling again either."

Did she just say the day I become an O'Reilly? My heart picks up pace, and I teeter on the edge of panic and sheer glee. The thought both excites me and scares me beyond words. We sit quietly for a few minutes finishing our tea before she stands and grabs her purse.

"I'll leave you to your day. I hope I didn't intrude."

"Not one bit. You stop over whenever you like. Thank you for the talk."

Reaching the door to my apartment, Siobhan leans in and fully takes me into her arms. Her embrace resembles nothing of my mother's. When my mother would hug me, she would place a hand on each of my upper arms and place her cheek against mine briefly while throwing a fake kiss that never touched my skin. This was a hug that I always wanted but never got. The one I still want for some unknown reason from my mother. But for now, I'll take this one.

Stepping back, she smiles as I open the door for her. Before she disappears from the doorway, she turns to me. "You have a new beginning. One that is yours to do whatever it is that makes you happy. Only you have that power."

*   *   *

AFTER SIOBHAN LEFT, I spend the rest of the day cleaning the apartment from top to bottom. I cook dinner from scratch for the first time in probably a year. I've decided to talk to Finn about Kael, but as the day progresses, I start to get more worried about Finn not calling or texting me. I text him a few times and get no answer. At eight o'clock, I text him again.

ARE you coming to stay over tonight?

STARING AT MY PHONE, my palms begin to sweat, fearing his lack of response. Then my phone pings.

No.

THE SINKING feeling dives from my throat into my already broken heart, then straight into my stomach. I've done this. I pushed him away at the pub just like I did before. Not having the slightest idea of what to do, I go to Leigh. She's got to have some advice of how I can fix this or how to get over it. I'm so lost I'm not sure which one. I swing open my door to march to hers, but Ryan is standing there with his hand up as if he was about to knock.

"How did you get up here without me buzzing you in?" I ask.

Ryan scratches the back of his head. "Well, some lady was walking out as I came up to the building and held the door open for me. Probably not that safe."

"What are you doing here anyway? I told you I was busy for the next few days."

"You want to go get a drink? I really need a fucking drink."

"That doesn't answer the question."

"I've just had a bad few days living at that house. Can we please just go get a drink?"

Fuck. Maybe a few shots would help me straighten out this mess in my head.

"Yeah, I'll go, but I'm not changing. You're going to have to deal with being seen with a sweaty emotional mess."

"Whatever. Let's just go."

Ryan and I sit at the bar of a local dive, spilling our guts to one another. He tells me that he has plans to propose to Ally, but he's been worried lately because it seems like she's pulling away from him. The entire time all I can think about is Finn feeling like I'm doing that to him. When Ryan's done telling me about what's going on with him, I tell him all about Kael and Finn's family.

I take another shot of Jameson on our way to play one game of darts before we head home.

My body is full of tingles and the lines in the sidewalk look crooked. I'm so happy when we reach my building. I hand Ryan my key to open the door. The stairs are an entirely new beast. Ryan keeps shushing me as my drunken laughter echoes in the stairway. We reach the door to my apartment, but before Ryan can get the key into the door, I trip and almost fall. His arm shoots out and catches me. He steadies me against the wall next to the door. His body presses against mine. Suddenly, I feel something on my side. Looking down, I see Ryan's hand is up my shirt.

"Ally," he mumbles. My vision becomes blurry before it turns to darkness.

CHAPTER TWELVE

THE DOWN PILLOW is soft under my head as the morning light shines in through the window. Still tired, I stretch but quickly retract from the ache surging through my body. My eyes bolt open as I sit up and take a look around the room that isn't mine. Flinging my feet out of the covers and placing them on the cold hardwood floor, I stand and immediately regret it. The pain shoots through my head.

"Ooohhh shit," I curse, holding my head tightly with both hands. Suddenly, the door opens.

"Well, nice to see my little lush has awoken from her peaceful drunken dumbass stupor."

"Leigh, how the fuck did I end up in your guest bedroom? And why are you cussing like that?"

"I saw you and Ryan come home last night. Actually, I heard you. I'm sure the entire building did, too."

"Oh, great. Another moment to be proud of," I say, rolling my eyes and collapsing back onto the bed. "So, how did I end up in your apartment instead of mine?"

"Ryan is in your apartment."

"So?"

"Do you remember anything from last night?" Leigh's voice is stern, except Leigh's stern voice is like most people's regular voice.

"I remember walking home, but after that, it's a little fuzzy. Why?"

"Let's just say, I saved your ass last night and you will owe me for the rest of your life. Like you're paying for Chinese forever."

"What the hell are you talking about?"

"I heard you coming up the stairs last night. So I got out of bed and went to check on you. When I opened my door…" Leigh hesitates, and I become scared to hear the rest. "Ryan had you against the wall with his hand up your shirt."

"What?" I yell, pacing Leigh's guest bedroom.

"I yelled for him to stop and he did. He was obviously as drunk as you were. So I got him into your apartment where he quickly passed out, and Carter carried you into ours. After what I saw, there was no way in hell I was leaving you alone with him while you were drunk."

The thought of Ryan having his hands on me, in that way, makes my stomach turn.

"Holy shit. I think I'm going to be sick."

"Now calm down. Nothing happened. Just don't forget. Chinese for life." She winks at me, pats my head, and walks out of the room. Thank God for Leigh. If she hadn't stopped Ryan, who knows what would have happened. The light gets brighter as I walk into the living room, guided by the smell of maple pancakes and bacon. On a regular day, I'd do just about anything for Leigh's homemade pancakes. They may even be slightly better than my sugar and cinnamon squares. But today, I'm afraid if I eat something, it won't stay in me for long.

"I'm going home. Thank you for having my back."

She smiles as she places cut up pancakes in front of Landon.

"One piece of advice?" she asks as if she's not going to give it to me whether I want it or not. "Don't tell Finn."

"Finny, Finn, Finn! I like Finny, Finn, Finn," Landon shouts, his mouth overcapacity with pancakes.

"You taught him to say that, didn't you?" I look to Leigh, accusing.

"Perhaps I said it a time or two."

As usual, sweet little Leigh's smirk could put the proudest sinner to shame. Shaking my head, I wrap my arms around her and quickly squeeze.

My apartment door has never looked so daunting. It's always been my safe haven, the place where I could escape all my problems and people in my life. But I've never wanted to run away from this place more than I do right now. Trying to find the right words, I stall and trace the numbers 201 that are attached to the door. How do I even begin a conversation like this? Feeling like I've delayed enough, I straighten my shoulders, take a calming breath, and walk in. Ryan looks like he feels pretty bad, but he forces a smile in my direction as he continues to fold the blanket he slept with last night and places it on the arm of the couch.

"Hey, I'm glad you're here."

Uh oh. Apparently, I should have taken a few more calming breaths before I came in here.

"You are?" I ask.

"Yeah, we have to talk and then I've got to head back to Albany. I've got a dinner meeting later."

Ryan takes a seat on the couch and smacks the cushion next to his for me to come sit down.

"Uh, why don't we sit at the table?" I quickly move to the dining room table, feeling like it will save me from having to be too close to Ryan for this talk. Luckily, he comes over without much fuss and sits across the table from me. I wait for Ryan to start talking because up to this point, I'm still not sure what to even say.

"What time did you go over to Leigh's this morning? Must have been early."

Damn. I'm going to have to start this.

"Look. I think I was a little too drunk last night. I hope I didn't give you the wrong idea."

"The wrong idea? What are you talking about?"

"You don't remember, do you?"

"Remember what? Daphs, stop screwing with me."

"Last night, Leigh came out of her apartment to see us in the hallway right outside my apartment. You had your…you had your hand up my shirt," I spit out. "She stopped you and put you in here and me over there."

"You're fucking lying."

"Are you serious right now? Why would I lie about something like that?"

"Oh God."

"That's what I'm saying."

"Let's forget that ever happened. I need to talk to you about something."

My eyes stretch wide as I stare, dumbfounded. "That's it? That's all you have to say about it? What about Ally?"

"What? You said nothing happened. So what am I supposed to be upset about? I have something bigger to talk to you about right now."

This sounds serious and maybe he's right. Nothing happened, so no need to feel guilty about it. *Right?*

"What is it?" I ask Ryan.

"One couple has been in the house three times and the realtor told me they like it a lot and are seriously contemplating putting in an offer."

All the air is pushed right out of my lungs.

The thought of someone else living in the house that Jarrod loved so much makes me miserable.

"That was bound to happen, right? We'll have to let it go sooner or later," I say quietly.

"I have a proposition for you," he says unexpectedly. "I want to buy the house. I'll give you full asking price. No negotiations. I don't need an inspection."

The breath slowly returns to my chest and a little excitement emerges. I would rather have Ryan in that house than anyone else. Jarrod loved having him there and I know he would approve.

"But there's a condition," he adds.

"Oh?"

"You have to be okay with me completely remodeling the house. As in, it probably won't be recognizable on the inside. It will still have all of the memories and be the same space, just different."

I wasn't expecting that. The thought of the inside of the house being gone forever is a little depressing. On the other hand, if a stranger moved in, I'd never see it again anyways.

"No."

"No?" Ryan asks, disappointed.

"You're not paying full asking price. I'll find out what the payoff is for the current mortgage. You pay that price. Jarrod would have wanted it done that way, so don't argue."

Ryan stifles a little sniff. "I know it's going to take a while for the sale to be completed, but I have a problem. I can't stay in that house anymore the way it is. Everywhere I turn, I see Jarrod standing against the counter or look for his jacket to be thrown over the back of the couch. So either I have to move out until the sale is final, or I'd like to start the remodel as soon as possible. It's up to you. I'm not trying to give you an ultimatum. I just can't live there anymore the way it is."

I thought I was going to walk in here and have to tell Ryan that I'm not into him. I was dreading that conversation. Now I wish we were having that talk. This one is worse.

"I don't want the house empty. So I guess you can start." Ryan nods then his head dips down into his lap.

"There's one more thing."

"Jesus, I don't think I can take one more thing, Ryan."

"I've already moved all of my things out. All that's left in the house is Jarrod's. Do you want to go through it? If it's too hard for you, I can take care of it."

"No. I'll come tomorrow and figure it all out. I'll call my mother and let her go over there first. She can take what she wants."

Ryan and I sit quietly, sulking at the dining room for a long time. The silence is trying to heal us, but it's not working.

When Ryan looks to his watch, he rises from the table and stops right next to me, placing his hand on my shoulder.

"We'll get through this, Daphs. I mean, Daphne. I know you hate me calling you that, and I've tried not to, but it's just a habit. It's the only way I ever heard Jarrod say your name."

He walks to the coffee table to pick up his wallet and keys.

Attempting to calm myself, I take long deep breaths, but it's coming and it's unstoppable this time. I catapult out of my chair and run to Ryan, throwing my hands around his neck and cry. I cry hard. He doesn't let me go until I've calmed down, which takes longer than usual.

"Are you okay?" he asks as my grip on him loosens and we separate.

"Yeah. I'll be okay."

Ryan opens the door to my apartment and turns to me just as he's walking out.

"Bye, Daphne."

"Please don't stop calling me Daphs. Otherwise, I'll never hear it again."

I can tell Ryan is barely holding it together so he just smiles and nods as he closes my door.

Herman has come out of hiding and is now meowing at my feet. He follows me the entire way to the closet where his food is and then to his bowl. Once food is involved, he's not interested in me anymore until he has a full belly.

I don't want to, but I have to call my mother. As usual, I'm sure she won't answer, but he's her son. It wouldn't be fair of me not to tell her about the sale of Jarrod's house. So, I hike up my big girl panties and call my mother. I talk to Herman as the phone rings but silence as soon as I hear my mother's voice.

"Daphne?"

"Hello, Mother."

"Is there something you need?"

A silent and sarcastic snicker emerges from me by her immediate need to get to the point.

"Yes. I'm selling Jarrod's house to Ryan. He's going to completely renovate the inside of it so he has removed all of his personal belongings. He needs the house empty, so I'm going there tomorrow to figure out what to do with Jarrod's belongings. I thought you might want to go there tomorrow morning and take what you want before I get there."

I'm surprised to hear a sniffle that I know my mother didn't intend for me to hear.

"I'll go over in the morning. Is there anything else?"

"That's all."

"Goodbye, Daphne."

"Bye, Mom."

The usual coldness from my mother isn't surprising. But hearing her get emotional is. How much is she actually hiding?

I'm positive that I smell like stale alcohol and sweat, so I take a quick shower and collapse onto my bed, covering myself up all the way past my head. I'm glad it doesn't take long to fall asleep.

* * *

THE FRONT DOOR opening startles me awake and I realize someone is in my apartment. It doesn't last long before my bedroom door opens, which puts me on full alert.

"Daphne." The sound of his voice relieves me.

"Here," I say from under the covers, and Finn comes rushing to me.

"You okay?" he asks curtly.

"Somewhat," I admit. "Why?"

Finn sits on the edge of the bed. His hands cup my cheeks as he places the most peaceful kiss on my lips.

"Are you about done with pushin' me away? I've tried to give you some distance. But I can't take it anymore. I'm not goin' anywhere, I don't care how hard you try."

"You ignored me for two days. I thought you already left."

"Leavin' isn't my style, Daffodil. I just needed to be set straight."

"Set straight? Who did that?"

"The wisest woman I know."

I smile knowing I'll need to thank Siobhan later.

"Wait, why did you ask me if I was okay?"

"You didn't show up to work."

I quickly reach for my phone to see that I'm two hours past the start of my shift.

My head flies backwards. "Shit," I mutter. "I forgot all about working today." Flinging back the covers, I try to get out of bed, but two heavy arms that I've missed terribly hold me in place.

"It's okay. You look like you need to rest. I already got your shift covered for tonight." He pushes my legs back onto the bed and covers me with the blankets.

"No, I'm fine. I should get up anyways."

"You don't look fine. Not tryin' to be an asshole here, but you look like you've been cryin'."

"How do you know I've been crying?"

Finn reaches over to the nightstand and picks up a handful of crumpled up tissues and walks to the other side of the room to throw them in the trash can.

"Oh," I say shamefully.

"There's never a reason not to tell me the truth, Daffodil."

Oh shit. The truth. Suddenly, all I can think about is the fact that Ryan had his hand up my shirt last night. Even Leigh told me not to tell Finn, but now all I have is guilt and I'm full of it. If he finds out somehow, I think he would be more pissed off that I didn't tell him. Oh, fuck. Here I go.

"So I have something to tell you, but you can't go crazy."

His eyes immediately pelt me. "Tell me."

I hesitate and bite my bottom lip as if my teeth are trying to keep my lips shut. "I spent the night at Leigh's house last night."

He leans his head forward, looking for what the big deal is. "So?"

"She made me."

"Why would Leigh make you stay at her place?"

"Ryan..." The minute his name left my mouth, Finn's body stiffened. "Ryan was here last night and we went out for a couple of drinks."

Finn eyes me from the side when I pause. "Keep going."

I take a breath and let it loose. "I remember walking home, but I'm pretty sure I blacked out after that." My favorite characteristic of Finn's face is showing, but it's not because he's smiling. The muscles in his jaw are so tight that it's causing his dimple to appear with every tick.

"How did you get to Leigh's?"

"She said I woke her up because I was loud coming up the stairs. When she opened her door to check on me, Ryan…"

Finn's teeth clench together. "Ryan what?"

"Ryan had his hand up my shirt."

Abruptly, Finn turns and walks out of my bedroom.

"Finn!" I yell.

"I'll fuckin' kill him!" his voice reverberates through my apartment as he walks out and slams my front door.

Oh my God. He actually might kill Ryan. Why don't I ever just listen to Leigh? Ignoring all signs of my hangover, I jump out of bed and go running after him. I get no response other than the echoes in the stairwell from me screaming Finn's name. I push open the building door and step out onto the stoop just in time to see Finn's Wrangler come tearing out of the parking garage and fly down the street. *FUCK*.

The sounds of the city street are muffled as my brain tries desperately to think of something. He's so upset I'm pretty sure that he wouldn't even answer his mother's phone call if she tried. *Oh c'mon! Think, Daphne!* A horn sounding off startles me, and at the same time, I know what to do. I race into the building and up to my apartment. Grabbing my phone, I find the person I need and press CALL.

"Hello?"

"Sophie…I…"

"Daphne? Are you okay? What's going on? Do you need help?"

God bless this woman and her beautiful heart.

"Finn. Please call Finn and calm him down. He's in his Wrangler and he's headed for trouble. I told him Ryan put his hand up my shirt last night and Finn's going to kill him!"

"Oh my God. Try not to panic, I'm on it. I'll call you." Sophie hangs up and my hangover returns fiercely and a sound of evil comes from my stomach. I run to the bathroom and throw up. I've never been this sick over just alcohol. I don't know what the hell has been going on every time I have a drink. Maybe as I'm getting older, it's just hitting me differently.

Gingerly I make my way to the kitchen and make a cup of peppermint tea to try to soothe my pissed off stomach. It's not helping that I haven't heard from Finn or Sophie yet. Once I'm situated on the couch with my tea, I can't wait any longer, so I call Sophie again.

"Daphne, I'm still on the other line. He's calming down, but he's not stopping yet. He's determined to drive to Albany. Benson and Paul are driving in his direction and trying to catch up to him. They'll make sure he doesn't do anything stupid. I'll call you back when I find out what's happening next. Siobhan has been here all day and is trying to talk some sense into him, too. I hope you're prepared. You've got yourself one of the biggest, stubborn-headed mules there is. I'll call you back. Okay, love?"

"Okay. Thank you, Sophie," my voice cracks.

Sophie giggles, "When a man gets like this, he's all in. Only thing you're missing right now is a ring. Well, welcome to the family."

As she disconnects, I can't even give myself the proper time to panic over the thought of marriage. The thought of Finn and what he's about to do to Ryan has me scared. *Shit! Ryan!* It'd probably be a good idea to warn him! Going back to my phone, I call him quickly.

"Hey, Daphs," Ryan greets

"Uhhh Uhhhh, I would be careful."

"What? Why?"

"I told Finn you had your hand up my shirt last night, and now, he wants to kill you."

"Oh shit! He could knock me out with his pinky finger," Ryan says as he's freaking out.

"Yes, I know. That's why I'm calling you. He's currently driving in your direction so maybe, if I were you, I'd hide until someone can stop him. I have his family on it. I'll call you later."

I pace my living room, not knowing what to do, when it dawns on me that maybe Kael can help. I grab my purse and rush out of the door.

The pub is packed, and I see Regan behind the bar, along with a few of the usual waitresses. Walking through, I don't see Kael though. Tasha goes flying past me, nearly spilling the glass of ale she has.

"Tasha," I yell to her. "Where's Kael?"

"Office!"

Knowing that Finn is gone, I knock on the office door.

"Come in."

As I enter the room, Kael is on the office phone. He gives me an annoyed look and then motions for me to sit in the chair across the desk.

"Stop being a complete dumbass. You're scaring the hell out of Daphne," he shouts into the phone. "Yes. I'm looking right at her and she looks pale as a ghost." Kael stands up and shuts the door that I left open and then returns to his chair. "Yeah? Good." Kael abruptly hangs up the phone, then stares at me.

"What's good?" I hesitate to ask.

"Benson and Paul were in his rearview, and he is pulling over. He'll listen to them."

I angle my head in guilt, and a tear streams down my cheek.

"Don't do that. Finn would lose whatever he has left of his mind if he finds out you were sitting in here crying." Kael sighs loudly. "I'm not a fan of this relationship, you know that. But my brother is so in love with you, he can't even see straight. I haven't seen him this upset since—well, I've never seen him this upset. Even Mel leaving didn't affect him like this. I heard what happened last night and I can't say that I blame him for losing his shit. But maybe you should think about not drinking so much."

"That's just it, Kael!" I yell through my tears. "I haven't been drinking anything different or more than I have before. I've never blacked out or been this sick after I've gone out. I don't get it. I had shots last night, but nothing that I would've blacked out from."

Kael sits forward in the chair and I'm struck by how similar his facial features are to Finn's. He's missing the coveted dimple, but his jaw ticks the same. I'm not sure how I've never noticed this before. Then again, my sights have always been focused on Finn.

"Do you remember what you had?"

"Yeah. I had an Irish Redhead and three shots of Jameson. It's what I order every time I go out," I say, throwing my hands up in frustration.

"Didn't you black out before last night, too?"

"Yes, I don't understand what's going on with me."

"Wasn't Ryan with you those times, too?"

"Yeah, what are you getting at?"

Kael's eyes squint as the tick in his jaw gets more profound. He picks up the phone and forcefully punches numbers into the keypad, then puts the receiver up to his ear.

"I was wrong. Go kill that fucker." My eyes widen and the confusion soars through me. "You know how she's been blacking out? Yeah, I think he's slippin' roofies into her drinks."

I fly back into my seat when Finn's screaming voice is loud enough for me to hear. As soon as his voice silences, Kael hangs up the phone.

"I think it's safe to say that Finn won't be home anytime soon."

"Why would you do that? Ryan would never do that to me. Why would you send Finn into danger like that? He could get hurt or go to jail! What would I do without him?" I yell before I collapse into my hands, tears flowing.

Through my sobbing, the sound of Kael's shoes come from around the desk and stop in front of me. He kneels at my feet and forces my face up with his finger under my chin.

"You just convinced me."

"What?"

"All I've seen is Finn devoting himself to you, committing himself to this relationship, and you seem so closed off. So cold. But you really love him, don't you?"

I sniffle and my breath hiccups as I try to speak. "More than I ever knew I was capable of."

"Then I'll bail him out. No one does that to this family." A smile spreads across his face like he's real pleased with himself.

"Stop him, please." My hand reaches out grabbing onto Kael's arm.

"Don't worry. He'll be fine. Benson and Paul won't let Finn kill him. But if I had to guess, they aren't going to be too happy with that news either."

Knowing that Benson and Paul are with Finn makes me feel a little bit better. At least he isn't alone and making rash decisions.

"Why don't you head home? Let him figure this out," Kael tells me, then leaves the office.

Knowing there's nothing I can do sulking in the office at the pub, I leave. As soon as I get outside, I call Ally.

"Hello?" Ally answers.

"Are you with Ryan?"

"No, why?"

"Are you in Boston?"

"I'm in New York for meetings. Daphne, this bride wants everything in crystal," she says, her voice squeaking with excitement before cutting to serious. "Why, is something wrong?"

"No, everything is fine." I assure her. I'm not going to be the one to tell her that her boyfriend had his hand up my shirt or that my boyfriend is now wanting to kill him. Or that they all think that Ryan roofied me. I don't believe that for one second though.

"I just wondered when you were coming back to town so we could hang out again," I lie.

"Oh girl, we're going to have to soon. I want to go back to that home store to buy the other candlesticks and centerpieces we saw. I'll text you when I get back to Albany."

"That sounds good."

"Bye."

"Bye, Ally."

I walk back to my apartment to get cleaned up since I ran out after Finn in the clothes I slept in. Sick of waiting and needing to hear his voice, I try to call Finn, but he doesn't answer so I text him instead.

I'm worried. I love you.

Immediately I get a response that settles me down.

Don't be. We are talking with Ryan now. He's fine I promise. I'm coming over as soon as we get back into town, but it will be late. Love you, too.

I text Leigh to see if she wants to hang out so I'm not alone to analyze everything that's happened today, but she texts back that they aren't home. So, that leaves me and my sugar and cinnamon squares to watch all the reality TV I possibly can before Finn comes back.

The apartment gradually gets darker until the only light in the place is from the TV. Herman is barely visible on top of my favorite black blanket in between my legs as I lay on the couch. By the fourth rerun of the *Golden Girls*, my eyelids can no longer stay open no matter how hard I try to force them to. I want to see him. I want to see Finn walk through this door so I can find out what happened with Ryan and stop worrying about him driving all the way back from Albany. He's probably not going to be too happy when he finds out I'm going to be driving there tomorrow.

I jolt as arms hold me close against a bulky hard body.

"I've got you, Daffodil."

I press my face deeply into his neck as he carries me to bed. Placing me gently in the middle, he climbs in right behind me. The scent of bergamot invades my nose and I realize that he's already showered and is in just his boxers.

"What happened? Ryan?" I mumble still half asleep.

"Shhh, he's fine. We'll talk about it tomorrow."

Finn leans over my body, and his lips enclose soft but deep on mine. He lingers as my hand sleepily touches the back of his neck. He kisses me again before settling on his back, pulling me into his side, my head resting on his chest. I'm thankful for the peace Finn brings me. Tomorrow is going to be one of the hardest days I've had since the day my brother died.

CHAPTER THIRTEEN

THE TEA KETTLE whistle blares for the third time this morning. I had black tea to wake up, followed by peppermint tea to calm my nervous stomach. I'm awake, but my stomach is still in knots knowing what I have to do today.

"Hey," Finn says from the doorway of the bedroom.

I'm also not excited to tell Finn I have to go to Albany today, so I just flash him a fake smile, but he knows me too well to buy it.

"You okay? You've been in a daze for over two minutes."

"No I haven't." I try to blow off his intuition.

"I've been standing here watching you and you didn't even notice me. Or the kettle that's been ready for a minute."

Finn walks to the kitchen, grabs the kettle, and pours some of the boiling water into my mug.

"What happened with Ryan?"

"He might be a little sore today, but he's fine."

"What do you mean, sore? What did you do to him?"

"I may have knocked the wind out of him and perhaps bruised a rib or two."

"Finn," I yell. "I told Kael, there's no way he would roofie me. He wouldn't do that to my brother."

"I know. I cleared all of that up before I punched him. If I would've thought he did that, he'd be in the hospital. I can tell ya he won't be drinking with you anymore though."

"The only thing I can think of is that I've been so overwhelmed with emotion and exhaustion that maybe I just can't handle the liquor like I used to."

"Anyway," Finn says, obviously changing the subject. "Why are you awake so early? The sun is barely up."

"I have to go to Albany today. I'll be back tomorrow."

"What?" Finn asks, surprised.

"Ryan is buying Jarrod's house. I have to go figure out what to do with all of my brother's belongings. I assume it will take time, so I booked a hotel."

"I'll get a shower and then we'll go." Finn turns toward the bathroom.

"No. Your parents are leaving tomorrow and you need to be here with them."

"They'll understand."

"Finn, please. I don't want to be the reason you don't say goodbye to your family. Kael will be furious if you leave him alone again at the pub. I can do this. As long as I can call you later and hear your voice, I'll be okay. Tell your parents goodbye for me?"

I know by Finn's expression he doesn't want me to go alone, but he knows I'm right.

"Call me when you get there?"

"I promise."

* * *

PULLING up to the white house that used to represent the only thing I knew about home, my heart is crushed. The flowers that used to be vibrant and welcoming are now dried, brown leaves. The crisp green yard that Jarrod was so proud of is now full of weeds and is a lifeless shade of yellow. I sit in the driveway for thirty minutes, trying to make myself get out of the car. Instead, I back out and decide to go to lunch first.

The local diner was a place I visited daily when I stayed with Jarrod. Too heavy-hearted to eat, I stare at the scratch on the table and sip coffee. Coffee is the most disgusting liquid to ever hit my taste buds, but I drink it anyway. Over half of it is sugar and milk, but the coffee taste is still there. My phone rings in my purse. *Shit.* I'm not doing a very good job at keeping my promises.

"Finn, I'm so sorry."

"It's okay. You okay?"

"Yeah, I'm having coffee at a diner close to Jarrod's."

"You're drinking coffee?"

"It's gross," I giggle.

"How's it going in the house?"

"I haven't been inside yet."

"Daphne, you've been gone for five hours."

My voice quiets as I admit the truth. "I just can't go in yet."

Finn's sigh is loud, and Kael's concerned voice comes from the background. "I knew I should have come with you," Finn says.

An older, well-dressed man enters the diner and catches my eye.

"Daddy?" I blurt loudly.

"What?" Finn questions.

"My dad," I breathe. "I gotta go."

Without saying goodbye or waiting for a response from Finn, I hang up the phone. I can't take my eyes off of the tall man that just walked in. His body turned to me as soon as I called his name.

"Baby? Oh my girl," he exclaims as he hustles in my direction. I step out of the booth and am taken aback by the force of my dad putting his arms around me and squeezing hard. As he loosens his grip and we back away from each other, a tear slides down his cheek. I motion to the empty side of the booth, inviting him to join me. It's been years since I've seen him.

"Your mother—"

"I don't want to talk about her right now. Why haven't you called? Or visited?"

"Baby, you know your mother is a difficult woman."

"That shouldn't stop you from having a relationship with your kids. You don't need her permission to talk to me. It's not an excuse."

I don't want this chance meeting to turn into a bash on my dad. I'm glad to see him, but his absence has affected me. It changed the way I view the world. I've never been given the time to tell him how I feel. I want him to know that I love him and he's welcome in my life. But I'm still so angry.

"I know it's not an excuse. But I saw you. When you would come to Albany, I would see you around town. It was hard for me to stay away, but your mother convinced me that we would just bring you down like we did Jarrod. She made it sound like you were going to be better off without us, and I believe her."

I flinch at the confirmation. I always knew it was all her. Since I can remember, my dad has let my mother keep us apart. My mother has pushed my dad around and told him what to do, how to act and what to say since the day he slipped that wedding band on his finger. Maybe that's why I never held it against him perhaps as much as I should have. I know how difficult she can be. Yet I still feel like there's something I don't get. How can a man allow someone to keep him from his children?

"I wish you would work it out with your mother." My father's face has aged drastically since I last saw him. The years have not gone easy on him and it looks as though he carries his burdens on it. Even from across the table, the familiar scent of his hair pomade brings me back to the time I used an entire can of it on my dolly. His hair, although gray now, is neatly combed to the side, and his mustache is trimmed perfectly, just as I remember it always being. He opens the button on his tailored black suit and leans in.

"It's all up to her. She's always been the one to push me away, and I've been the one trying. As I get older, I don't want to try anymore." It hurts to admit this out loud but it's true. For many years I've tried to make my mother want me.

His phone chimes and he lifts his hand, looking at his watch.

"Baby, you know I hate to do this to you, but I have a meeting with a high-risk client back at the office."

"No," I blurt. "I haven't seen you in years. I'm not ready for you to go yet."

His expression looks as hurt as my heart. "I can't help it. I have to go." He stands, buttoning up his suit jacket. "Your mother told me you are selling Ryan the house. I think Jarrod wouldn't have wanted it any other way. He'd be proud of you. I know I am."

My body is frozen to the seat from his last words as he kisses the top of my head and brushes his thumb along my cheek.

"I love you, baby."

"I love you too, Daddy."

Confused as to how he could leave me so easily, I watch him walk out of the diner and get into his Mercedes. Unable to sit in this booth without crying from the odd encounter with my father, I call the waitress over, pay my bill, and get the hell out of the diner.

I drive right past Jarrod's house and head to my hotel instead. I wasted so much time in the diner that I look to my phone and remember that I practically hung up on Finn. I find his name and call him.

"You okay?" he answers after the first ring.

"I'm good. I talked to my dad. It was short but good."

"He make you upset?"

"No," I lie.

"Hmm. That doesn't sound like…"

"I don't want to talk anymore. I love you, Finn," I blurt out, interrupting him.

"Love you, too."

I can tell Finn was reluctant to hang up. I'm just trying to keep it together and if I go into detail, I'll lose it for sure.

I waste as much time as I can before the time comes that I have to go to Jarrod's. There's no more time to put it off. I haven't even begun to think about what I'm going to do with all of his stuff. I know there are a few things I want to put in storage until I can get them Boston. I take each step at a snail's pace to my car. Once inside, I turn the key, fasten my seatbelt, and give myself a stern look in the review mirror.

"You can do this."

* * *

SHUTTING the door to my car takes more effort than I thought it would after I parked in the driveway. The last time I was in this house, I saw my brother's beautiful smile. One that I'll never see again. I put my key in and open the door.

As the space comes into view, the deep pang in my chest is suffocating. It's empty. Everything is gone. The couches that Jarrod and I shopped for a week straight to find. Gone. The curtains that we found to match perfectly are striped from the windows, leaving them with only blinds. The sign I hung up in the main living room that said "YOU ARE LOVED" is no longer there, leaving only the nail head sticking out from the wall.

My purse falls from my arm. My mouth opens in shock. I continue my torturous walk through. I have no doubt that my mother emptied this house. She took everything. Who knows where any of it ended up. The only thing I know is that it's all gone. All of the bright yellow accents Jarrod and I bought for his kitchen to keep it cheerful have disappeared. I stand in the empty spot where the large rectangular dining room table was. It was one of the pieces of furniture I really wanted to keep. Jarrod and I spent a lot of time doing puzzles on it. I could be looking for a piece for over an hour and he would sit down, pick it out of the pile of pieces, and put it in place. It would make me so mad. I catch myself smiling at the memory. My hand grazes along the wall where a rainbow dances. One of the crystal stars that I brought him from a little Boston crystal shop still hangs from above the kitchen window, catching the setting sunlight. There used to be two there.

Ringing echoes through the space from my purse by the door, but I can't bring myself to answer it. I don't think I could even get one word to come out of my mouth at this point. It only rings for a minute before I assume whoever was on the other end hung up or the voicemail kicked in. I continue down the hallway and into Jarrod's office. The only thing remaining in the cream-colored room is the indentations of Jarrod's dark cherry desk.

The void makes each step I take sound like a rumble of thunder through the open house. Just as I'm about to make the turn to head up the stairs, something catches my eye from the other side of the living room. I didn't see them when I came in. The pillows my mother hated because she said they didn't match Jarrod's décor. I pick one of them up and squeeze it against my chest. I'm thankful for something to hold onto, as I'm about to enter the place where my brother took his last breath.

By the time I reach the top of the stairs, I'm out of breath and courage. But there's no going back now. Standing at the top of the stairs staring at the open loft, I know I should have walked right back out of this house when I saw it was empty.

As I enter into the hollow shell of what used to be Jarrod's bedroom, the tears begin to stream down my face. Standing in the middle of this empty room, I stare at the door to the bathroom where it all ended. It's closed and there's no desire to open it. As heart wrenching as this is, a bizarre sense of peace suddenly comes me. I feel close to him in here. The pillow falls from my grip, and I follow it to the floor. Curling my body into a tight ball, the silence fades as my sobs echo against the walls.

Loud repetitive beeps jar me out of my tear-filled daze in the now darkening room. There's an odor of smoke.

"Oh my God," I say to the emptiness. "The house."

CHAPTER FOURTEEN

I RISE from the floor then fall straight back down, remembering I should stay low. Even though I can smell the smoke, I can't see it. On hands and knees, I crawl out of the bedroom and into the hall. It's dark and hard to tell exactly where the smoke is coming from, but it's definitely on the first floor. I manage to get closer to the loft banister as the smoke gets heavier. The sight looking down to the first floor below is something out of a nightmare. The orange flames from the kitchen becomes blinding as the fire grows before my eyes. I have to get out. I pull my shirt over my nose and mouth to filter some of the smoke from going into my lungs. I take a breath in, and then hold it while I scoot closer to the stairs. The loud beeping is now muzzled by a constant and deafening roar. I make it down a few steps when I stop, paralyzed by both terror and the strange beauty of the flames that are now at the bottom of the steps. In that moment, the raging inferno becomes silent. The blur of the flames dancing across the wall, creeping its way toward me, are hypnotic.

A deep cough shakes me from my trance and I realize that I've stood up. My eyes sting from the billowing smoke so I close them tightly. Through the crackling of wood burning, I hear something. A voice. It's faint and calling my name.

"Get out!"

I know that voice. *Jarrod?* Then, banging.

"Daphne!"

Finn? I force my eyes open and look over the banister. Finn is outside of the large picture window looking in. I try yelling to him, but nothing comes out except coughing. The room is starting to spin and I can't breathe. With the last bit of strength I have, I stand and witness the expression of horror on his face. "Daphne!" he screams as his fists break straight through the glass the same time my foot slips from the step. Falling in what feels like slow motion, all I can see are the flames roaring next to me. Pain shoots through my leg as I hit the bottom. Finn's familiar arms lift me from the floor and move quickly.

"I've got you, Daffodil," he barely gets out as he coughs.

Even though my eyes are closed, I can tell when the light turns from bright and hot to dim and cold. The air turns from heavy to weightless, and my head lifts as I'm lowered to the frigid grass. Sirens loudly blare behind me. But as my eyes become clear, I can't stop staring at this burning house. The house that my brother worked so hard to get. The house that killed him. The house that almost killed me. Up in flames.

An oxygen mask is placed over my mouth and nose as the EMT begins asking me questions. But I'm not sure I'm even breathing at this point. Numb, I turn to Finn. He also has a mask on his face. Everything is quiet, and the world slows around me. Firefighters look like a blur as they rush around us, battling the flames. There's no use. Right in front of my eyes, the house falls into nothing but a pile of burning rubble.

The sobs are uncontrollable. But again, my heart is conflicted. This house was special to Jarrod. But I get the sensation of release. As if my brother is no longer trapped here. The smoke dances and twirls up into the clear night sky. He's finally free. So am I.

It's then that my mind fully clears. I search for Finn, not remembering which side I saw him. The second our eyes meet, he drops the mask and reaches for me.

"Daffodil," he breathes into my ear.

"You saved me," I choke out.

A voice interrupts us and turning, there's man in an EMT uniform.

"We should get to you to the hospital."

"I'm not leaving until it's out."

"We shouldn't wait."

"I'm. Not. Leaving. Until. It's. Out."

I'm not sure if it was my face or Finn's behind me that convinced him to let us wait a little longer before going to the hospital. Together, Finn and I sit on the lawn like statues. Murmurs of voices start low but get louder as what seems like the entire neighborhood gathers behind us. All of us, watching the very last piece of my brother's life go up in smoke.

* * *

"IT'S BROKEN," the doctor says as he walks into the room carrying the X-ray of my foot and a few of my chest. He shoves them into the clip on the light board. "Right there." He points his pen at the crack in a bone in my ankle. "And right there." I roll my eyes. "And right there."

It doesn't even faze me. I could care less about my broken ankle at this point. I just want to get the hell out of here.

"Where is the man that came in here with me?" I ask.

"I'll go check for you," the nurse says as she leaves the room.

"You got lucky."

Lucky? I don't feel lucky at this moment.

"They're all clean breaks, so we'll give you a temporary splint, and then you'll need to follow up with an orthopedic doctor as soon as possible. Your tests all came back normal as well as both of your chest X-rays. You got out of that house in good time. After the nurse puts the splint on, I'll have her bring you the release papers to sign. But if you develop any further symptoms, immediately come back to the ER."

"Okay," I say, my voice hoarse. "Where are my clothes?" I ask. After the X-ray was done, I was handed a white jumpsuit to wear.

"They were handed over to the police, which is typical for the situation. Would you like to speak to someone? I can call a social worker to come talk to you if you'd like." The ER doctor looks to me concerned.

"No. I just want to see my boyfriend."

The doctor nods his head and steps to the side when we both hear the door open again. My head tilts back and my internal panic subsides. A loud exhale comes from deep within me. I reach for Finn who is wearing the same white jumpsuit I have on. The panic returns when I get a good look at him. His arms are both bandaged and he has a gauze pad tapped to his forehead.

"Are you okay?" I screech.

"I'm fine. Just a few cuts from the glass." Then he turns to the doctor. "How is her leg?"

The doctor looks to me and I give him a nod of permission. He shows Finn the films and the three places where the bones are broken. As soon as the doctor leaves the room, Finn turns to me, wraps me up in his arms, and squeezes.

"I couldn't do it. I heard your voice on the phone and I couldn't have you here alone. Thank God I got to that house in time." His forehead dips to press against mine. I brush my fingertips delicately along the rigid bandages on both of Finn's forearms, so not to hurt him.

"I'm beginning to think a normal life isn't in my realm of possibilities. And now, I'm starting to drag you down with me."

"What is normal? Normal is something made up. There is no normal life. Besides, you would hate living a life that you classify as normal. It would be fuckin' boring as hell."

He smiles then kisses my lips as a nurse walks in to put the splint on my foot. She hands us papers on how to care for our injuries and that we can go. As Finn pushes me in a wheelchair through the hospital, he hands me his cellphone and tells me to call a taxi since both of our vehicles are still parked by the street at what used to be Jarrod's house. In the middle of looking up the phone number to call the taxi, we suddenly stop moving.

"Uhm. Daphne?" Finn calls my attention.

"Yeah?" I respond, still focused on the phone.

"Daphne, look."

Lifting my eyes from the phone screen, I see him. He's here. Just like I knew he always would be if I needed him.

"Daddy," I cry out to my father as he rushes into the lobby.

His face showing both concern and relief. "What would I have done? What the hell would I have done if something happened to you?"

"The house, Daddy. Jarrod's house is gone."

"I know, baby. The neighbors called and told me they took you two away in an ambulance." He rushes to my side, folding me into his arms, and I notice a tear in the corner of his eye. When he lets go and stands back, I glance around looking for my mother.

"Where's Mom?"

My dad's face falls and his hand rubs his chin.

"When I left you earlier, I told her I saw you at the diner. She seemed jumpy and disappeared. She won't answer my calls."

"I wish I could say that surprises me," I state. Then Finn coughs from behind me.

"Daddy, this is Finn. Finn this is my dad, Harrold."

Finn reaches out his hand and shakes the hand of my father. Such a strange, yet beautiful sight.

"Come on," my dad says. "Let's get you two out of here."

My dad walks us to his Mercedes, and Finn helps me hobble into the car. Finn just about has his door shut when we hear a police officer calling to us.

"Need something?" Finn asks the officer.

"I'm Detective Keets. I need to get statements from both of you. Separately."

"Not without our lawyer present," my dad says firmly.

"I'm not waiting for a lawyer," I announce.

"But—"

"No." My curt response gets me a nod, then he and Finn step out of the car.

"Can you ask her in the car? She has a broken ankle and shouldn't be on it," Finn informs the officer.

"Of course."

Finn and my dad walk to the front of the car, and it warms my heart to see the two of them talking to each other. They both look back toward me as the detective asks me a string of questions. When he's done, my dad returns to the car while Finn has his turn with Detective Keets.

Finn shakes the detectives hand then sits in the front seat next to my dad. I catch a look that happens between the two of them. Finn pulls his phone out of his pocket and begins rapidly texting. After a minute of pounding the buttons on his phone, it chimes back immediately.

"You were right?" my dad asks Finn, quietly.

"I was right. Arson."

"What?" I blurt out so loud my dad jumps. "Arson? How do you even know that?"

"The type of questions they were asking. It's obvious they think someone started that fire."

"How do you know what kind of questions they would even ask?" I just can't believe that anyone would purposefully do that to my brother's house.

"Paul."

The minute Paul's name comes out of Finn's mouth I know that its possible. Even though Paul straightened his life out long ago, he knows a lot about bad things. Not to mention he's researched a lot about law enforcement and how things are investigated. I also happen to know that Paul is friends with some dangerous people.

"This just doesn't make any sense. Who would want to set that house on fire? Jarrod's house? He's gone, so what's the point?"

"Oh my God," my dad says under his breath.

"What?" I ask.

"Nothing. Don't worry about it. I'm going to drop you two off at your hotel. It's late, and I have an important meeting in the morning that I just remembered."

* * *

FINN GENTLY HOLDS onto my elbow to help me get out of the back seat. My dad comes around the car to Finn and shakes his hand. He leans into Finn, patting him on the back and he whispers something in Finn's ear. He turns to me and hugs me tightly. I take a deep inhale of the familiar pomade scent.

"I love you, baby. You've found yourself a real good one," he says as he nods in Finn's direction.

"I know," I agree, smiling at Finn. "I love you too, Daddy." The thought crosses my mind that this could be the last time I get this kind of response from my dad without my mother being around. The next time I talk to him might be months from now and the conversation will be as short and cut off as it's always been. At least I got this. I know how my daddy feels, and I'm not going to let anyone let me think any differently.

After watching the Mercedes disappear around the corner, Finn holds my arm as I struggle to manage the stupid ass crutches to walk into the hotel.

"Fuck this," Finn spits, and he swiftly wraps one arm around my back and one under the bend of my knees.

"Finn, put me down! You are going to hurt your arms even more. I can do it. Put me down right now."

He grunts and his face winces as my body puts weight on his injured arms.

"I can't. I can't fuckin' do it. I can't watch you struggle like that." He carries me all the way to the elevator, then to the room where I had dumped my bags earlier. I slide the card through the slot on the door. It blinks green, so I push the handle down so that Finn can kick the door open. He places me gently on the bed and quickly puts his hand under my ankle to guide it smoothly down. Once he's satisfied that my leg is positioned properly on a pillow, he hands me a pain pill and a water bottle. Lying with my back propped up against the headboard, I watch him pace the floor.

"Finn?" I whisper, but his head doesn't even turn in my direction. "Finn?" Again, nothing. "Finn!" I raise my voice in hopes of snatching him out of whatever horror scene he's seeing in his head. His eyes turn and meet with mine before he huffs and comes back to my side.

"I keep seeing you on the ground. Flames all around you."

"I'm okay. You saved me," I say sweetly while stroking his cheek with my thumb to prove that I'm all right, but his body doesn't loosen.

"They think someone did this. I'll fuckin' kill him."

"Shhh, they don't know anythi—"

His expression turns dark and haunting. "I'll. Fucking. Kill. Him."

"Why are you saying *him*? Do you know something I don't?"

"No." He gets back up from the bed and starts to pace again.

Unable to watch him torment himself all night, I twist and slide off of the side of the bed. Two steps and a yelp in pain is all it takes for Finn to scoop me up and put me right back on the bed again.

"Do I look like I need you hurtin' yourself right now?"

Desperate to feel him, to hear his heartbeat, to feel his love for me in his fingertips on my skin, I place my hand on his cheek and move my face so close to his I can feel his breath.

"Lay with me."

"I can't just pretend—"

"Lay with me," I whisper, my voice weak with the threat of tears.

He cups my face, closes his eyes, and kisses me softly. Carefully, he climbs in next to me. I snuggle deep into his side and place my head on his chest. There's nothing I want more than for this to all be a bad dream.

"Our clothes," I breathe.

"What?"

"They took our clothes."

"Paul said that's normal for an arson case. They're going to test them for accelerants."

"I can't believe this is happening." Not able to stay in this jumpsuit for one more minute, I angle myself up and pull it off of my arms. The nurse had pushed the pant leg up in order to secure the splint on my ankle. I look to Finn, unsure how to get my broken ankle out of it. The doctor said not to remove the splint for any reason.

"Well," Finn says, looking at my leg before he bends down and grabs ahold of the fabric. I watch the muscles bulge in his arms and shoulders as he rips the material right off of me. He takes his off and my eyes follow him to the trash can where he deposits them.

"I still can't wrap my head around what happened today," I admit. "It was the most glorious tragedy I've ever seen."

"Can I ask you somethin'?"

"Always," I respond.

"What were you thinking about on those stairs? It's like you were frozen in the middle of the fire."

I pause for a minute, contemplating if I should tell Finn the truth.

"I heard him." Finn's fingers never stop their pace as he gently strokes my arm. "I heard Jarrod say my name and then tell me to get out. Then, I heard you."

Finn kisses the top of my head and squeezes me gently. "What if I hadn't—?"

"You did," I interrupt. "All we need to focus on is that you did." Remembering what he said earlier in the car, I can't help but wonder if Finn has an idea of who would have wanted to burn down Jarrod's house. "Who do you think did this?" I ask quietly.

"I'll handle it."

Failing to hide it, the rage is obvious in his voice, and it terrifies me of what he might do.

"Don't do this. Don't leave me in the dark. I deserve to know everything."

Finn huffs as he shifts on the bed. "You're not going to like it."

"Please. Tell me."

"Let's just say, I know he's not in New York."

"*Ryan?* You think Ryan did this?" I ask. "No way. He loved that house just as much as Jarrod did. He was going to buy it. That makes no sense."

"I think it makes perfect sense. He wanted you, couldn't have you. Losing you and Jarrod was too much for him, and he just wanted to get rid of everything. All of his belongings were in a storage unit."

"I told you he was going to start renovations. That's why I came. I already knew his stuff was out."

"Don't you think it's a little strange that he didn't go to New York like he told you? He's been in Albany this entire time."

"How do you know where Ryan is?" I question, feeling angry and protective of the person my brother loved.

"Does it really matter?" Finn grumbles.

I sit up and turn to look at him, scolding. "Yes."

Finn runs his hands over his face. "Paul."

"I thought you said Paul doesn't do anything illegal anymore."

"He doesn't. But his friends do." Finn takes a hesitant pause. "Paul has been keeping close tabs on Ryan."

"What?" I snap. "This is going too far, Finn." Angry, I push myself off of Finn's body only to be hauled right back down again.

"You've become my entire world. I'm not about to let someone take that away from me. So if that means that I have someone keep an eye on Ryan to keep you safe, that's what I'm going to do."

"I think you're wrong, and when this is all said and done, you are going to owe him a huge apology."

"I hope you're right. For his sake."

CHAPTER FIFTEEN

"DAPHNE, WAKE UP."

Finn's voice pulls me into consciousness.

"What's the matter?" I ask, my voice gruff.

I squint, trying to see Finn's face, but it's taking longer than usual for them to focus. I grunt as the pain from my ankle surprises me.

"Your dad is on the phone."

Shocked, I sit up and take Finn's phone from him. Since my phone is a pile of melted metal, they must have exchanged numbers last night.

"Daddy?"

"Hey, baby. Wanted to see how you're feeling this morning."

"Meh. I've been better." I wince as Finn moves the pillows to accommodate my new position in the bed. I see his jaw pulsate in the corners and I know he's trying hard to keep himself under control. "Are you at work?"

"No. I'm just calling to tell you that I think you should stay away from Jarrod's. The police are done with both of your cars and I had them delivered this morning to the hotel. The front desk has your keys."

Suddenly, Finn's hand with pills appears in my face. I'm not taking those pain pills today. I can handle the pain, and I have a lot to do. I push his hand away and shake my head. Finn doesn't move, so I look in a different direction and continue to talk to my dad.

"Where is Mom?" I ask, but I'm not sure I want to know the answer. The last thing I need is the guilt of tearing the two of them apart. I know how much he loves her. Probably a lot more than she loves him.

"I'm not sure, baby." His voice is low and broken. "She hasn't been home, and she still won't answer."

It breaks my heart how lost he sounds without her. My feelings toward her have nothing to do with this. His heart still belongs to her and I don't want him to hurt.

"I need to talk to you about Ryan. He—"

"Daddy?"

"Victoria, you're home."

"Who's on the phone, Harrold?"

"It's Daphne, dear. Do you want to talk to her?"

"No. Tell her I love her. We need to go now. Hang up, Harrold."

Silence holds the line as my mouth has physically dropped open. I can almost picture my mother walking in casually, as if my dad hadn't been losing his mind all night. I wonder if she even knows about Jarrod's house. I'm sure that is going to be all my fault, too.

"I have to go, baby. I love you."

"Daddy, wait." My heart seethes from how quickly this turned.

"I love you, baby. Don't you ever forget that."

I continue to hold the phone up to my ear, minutes after my dad disconnected. Finn sits at the two-person table by the window, staring at me. I can tell he isn't sure what to say. Slowly, he rises and walks to me, taking the phone from my hand and shutting it off. He sits on the edge of the bed and pulls me closely as I cry. Again.

"You should probably eat," I say, wiping my face and sitting upright. A change in the conversation is necessary if I'm going to move on with my day.

"You need to eat, too. I'll order something."

"No. I need to go outside and get out of this room. Sulking is just going to keep the feeling constant."

"That ankle is supposed to be elevated. We're not going out."

Finn rises from the bed and opens the curtains wide. The morning sun pours into the room as I twist out of the bed and grab the crutches.

"What are you doing? Sit back down."

"I have to go to the bathroom. For crying out loud, Finn," I yell out of frustration.

Walking over, he grabs ahold of my arm to help me, which is only making moving the crutches harder. I know my sweet man just wants to help me. It's killing him to watch me like this. But he has to give a little.

"I'm strong. I've been through much worse than a broken foot. I promise you, if I need help, I will ask you for it."

Although his feet stay planted where I left him, his eyes have followed me the entire way to the bathroom.

I'm greeted by Finn leaning up against the wall across from the doorway as the bathroom door opens. I roll my eyes and move back in the direction of the bed with Finn directly behind me. I situate myself back on the bed and lean the crutches on the nightstand right next me.

"You tell me what you want to eat and we'll get it delivered."

Thinking fast, I come up with a plan.

"I've been craving something since I got into Albany. Jarrod and I used to get breakfast from there all the time."

"Great, what's it called?" Finn says, grabbing his phone.

"They don't deliver. Will you go pick it up for me, since you won't let me go there and eat it?"

"I'm not leaving you, Daphne."

"Please? It's the only thing that sounds good right now."

Finn puffs out a hesitant breath, then puts his phone down on the nightstand. Leaning over, he places a hand on either side of my body and brings his face close to mine.

"I'm going to take a shower, then I'll go out and get your food." He places a long kiss on my lips.

I nod, grab the TV remote, and put on the cooking channel. As soon as the door closes and I hear the sound of the running shower, I dial Ryan's number on the hotel phone.

"Hello?"

"Ryan. The house," my voice breaks.

"Holy fuck, Daphs. I heard everything. The neighbor called me. Are you okay?" he asks, breathless.

"I'll be fine. I broke my ankle on the stairs. Finn busted through the living room window and carried me out."

"Thank God. The cops have been all over me asking me weird questions. It feels like they think I set the house on fire. Why the fuck would I do that? How could I ever do that to Jarrod?"

"I know. Just keep complying with the police and they'll figure it out. It's going to be okay. Is Ally with you? Isn't her dad a lawyer or something?"

"Yeah, he's been over here helping me out. She was at a wedding in Florida, but she's on a plane right now headed back home. She's so freaked out. Fuck. They're here again. I've gotta go."

Just as I place the receiver into the cradle, Finn walks out of the bathroom. The hard muscles of his strong chest glisten with water droplets. His lower half is only covered by a white towel. The vision could drop me to my knees. I smile at him and signal for him to come closer to me with my finger.

"Who was on the phone?" he asks as he moves toward me, smirking at my demanding gesture.

"Front desk, booked another night."

"Good," Finn says as he reaches my body, and his hand runs up one of my legs over my torso and up to my neck. "Fuck, I want you. So bad. But I can't risk hurting you."

Shivers run through my body as his lips torment my nervous system.

"Soon. Soon, I won't be able to stop myself. I'm going to go."

He pulls away from me, and I know it's as painful for him as it is for me. Though it doesn't stop me from taking in every hard inch of his body as he dresses in front of me.

The half smirk appears with that dimple that makes me forget my own name as he walks to me. He kisses my lips and walks out of the hotel room. As soon as the door latches shut, I pick up the receiver and call for a taxi to pick me up. Poor Finn has no idea that I just sent him halfway across town. He'll be gone long enough.

Finn wants to protect me and keep me away from everything. But there are some things I have to do. I owe this to Jarrod.

Thankfully, I packed a shorts romper. It's loose enough to fit my splint through. Otherwise, I have no idea how I would have gotten my pants on without taking it off. I feel so guilty for tricking Finn. Even though the note I left him tells him I'll be back soon, I know he's going to be upset. As I make my way out of the hotel and into the taxi, all I can do is hope he'll forgive me later.

The taxi driver is a sweet older man named Smith. As we pull up to Jarrod's house, Smith gives me a confused look.

"Are you sure this is where you wanted to go?" Smith asks.

"I just want to see it. Can you park just for a minute? I'm not staying."

"Of course."

It's a struggle to try to get my crutches out of the car.

"Can I help you?" Smith asks, quickly opening his door. I smile as he grabs onto my elbow to help me out of the car. "You take your time. I'll wait."

"Thank you. I won't be but a minute."

He nods then returns to his car, shutting the door to give me privacy. I stop at the caution tape that is wrapped around the entire property. Staring at what's left of Jarrod's house, I still feel the same way I did last night. I'm sad that it's gone, but I don't feel him there like I did when I walked in yesterday. The front wall of the house is still intact, but the door is gone and it leads to nothing but a pile of ashes. The entire back of the house nothing but soot and burnt memories.

Slowly, I venture through the grass toward the backyard.

"I don't think you should be walking around here alone on those crutches," Smith says as he joins me at my side. "I'll walk with you."

"Thanks," I say with a sad smile as we walk. My crutch goes into a divot in the grass, and I stumble a bit to the side. Smith catches my arm and immediately rights me.

"You're all right," he says, nonchalantly letting me go again.

Once again at the front of the house, we stand on the sidewalk. Saying my final goodbye, I nod toward the house, then at Smith. He opens the taxi door for me to get in and takes care of my crutches. I take one last look at the house as we drive away.

* * *

"I'LL GO with you if you want," Smith says as we pull up to our second destination.

"You're so sweet, but I have to do this by myself. I'm not sure how long I'm going to be. It could be awhile, but I don't have a phone to call another taxi. I'll pay you for the entire time, just please don't leave."

"This trip is on me. Seems you need some good comin' your way. Maybe this will be the start. You take your time. I'll be here whenever you're done."

He gets out, hands me the crutches, and helps me to stand. From the road, you'd never know this was a cemetery if it weren't for the sign. Tall mature trees line the perimeter and all throughout the inside of the large graveyard. I'm not sure where Jarrod is at rest, so I begin walking along the trail, hoping to find his name. Hedges line the maze of headstones. Slowly, I come around the corner and see a woman sitting on a bench under a large mature sugar maple tree. Her hair is in a perfect chignon, she's wearing a light pink dress suit, and she's wiping tears from her long, haggard face.

I duck behind another large tree so she doesn't see me. Part of me wants to go to her. The other part of me can't handle the rejection. I watch her for a long time as she sobs and wipes her tears with tissue. Eventually, she stands up, presses her fingers to her lips, and then touches them to the headstone belonging to her son. Sluggish, she turns, and I listen to the echoes of her high heels clicking on the walkway as they get further away until they disappear completely.

Seeing my mother that way is maddening. Why couldn't she show Jarrod that love when he was here? It's been no secret to me that she has always had a softer spot for him. But never have we experienced the love she just showed a concrete headstone.

As soon as I'm sure my mother is gone, I hobble on my crutches to the place where my brother's body rests in the ground. Taking my mother's place, I sit on the bench under the umbrella of maple leaves. Having so much to say but not sure how to begin, I sit quietly for a minute. I listen to the song the leaves are singing in the warm breeze. My long hair blowing backward brushes against my skin, and a chill rocks my body.

"One word. The last thing I heard you say was only one word. How could you do that to me?" I ask the wind, my chin quivering. "I have so many questions I'll never get answers to. I was afraid to come back here. The fear is gone now, but I'm still not coming back. Not because I don't love you, but because you aren't here anymore. I know you're free. I felt it. I felt your sadness lift with that smoke. This is me, saying goodbye."

Leaving my crutches, I hobble to the headstone and painfully kneel. Staring at each letter in his name and the numbers telling his birth and death. Bending my head with one hand on the headstone, I let myself cry for my brother one last time before I move on, the way he wanted me to. A hand touches my shoulder and startles me. Through the glare of the sun dancing through the tree leaves, Smith's friendly smile appears and comforts me.

"Come on, dear. I'll take you home."

My breath hiccups as I nod, and Smith helps me off the ground. He hands me the crutches and we walk slowly back to the car.

As soon as I'm back in the taxi, I check my phone and see a bunch of frantic text messages from Finn. Seeing my mother at Jarrod's grave made me lose all sense of time. The phone pings again with another text message from Finn begging me to tell him where I am.

I'm okay. Just had something I needed to do. In a taxi on the way back to the hotel now. See you in a few minutes. I love you.

Pulling up to the hotel, I get a nervous feeling in my stomach. Finn is standing against the wall under the canopy of the front entrance. Smith gets out and makes it halfway around the car to help me out, but

Finn easily beats him. He flings the door open and pulls me out of the cab. His arms wrap tightly around me.

"Where did you go?" he asks, still holding on.

"I went to the house. Then I went to Jarrod's grave."

Finn leans back, his hand gripping the back of my neck as his eyes come even with mine. "I would have taken you."

"It was important for me to do this alone." I smile and lean my head further into his hand. He nods, understandingly and gently kisses my lips. A soft cough interrupts us. Smith is standing next to us, holding my crutches for me.

Finn tries to pay Smith but he refuses to take any money. The men shake hands and with a comforting smile and a soft nod, Smith gets into his taxi and goes on his way. It's a needed reminder of how great people can be when you least expect it.

Just as we enter the lobby, Finn's phone rings. He guides me to a chair and then moves slightly away from me as he answers it. I can't hear him, but his face is worried.

"Who was that?" I ask as he rejoins me.

"The police want to talk to you."

"It better not be about Ryan. He's been through enough. He didn't do this."

Finn doesn't say anything on the way to the police station. I'm not sure whether it's because he doesn't think Ryan really did it or if he does and doesn't want to fight with me about it.

As we enter the police department, Detective Keets stands tall against the counter, looking at papers inside of a file folder. He moves toward us with his hand extended.

"Hi, Daphne. How are you feeling?" he asks me, shaking my hand.

"I'm okay. Do you have news?" I ask him as he directs us into the nearest office.

He doesn't speak until we have all taken a seat.

"We've found evidence that suggests someone started the fire at your house."

Finn steps forward. "Yeah, we already assumed that from the questions you were asking. What are you doing to figure out who did it?" He's losing his patience, and this isn't the place to do it. "Have you looked into Ryan Margolis?"

"Finn!" I scold.

"We have questioned him at great length. At this time, he's not a suspect. We've received a few tips from some witnesses."

"There were witnesses? That's good, right?" I ask.

"Yes. It's very good. We have a description of a woman who was spotted around the house about an hour before your car was seen in your driveway. Do you know of any women that might want to harm you in any way?"

"Harm me? No," I say with certainty.

"What did she look like?" Finn asks.

"Short, had on jeans and a black hooded sweatshirt with a small yellow sun on the front right corner. The witness said she had long brown hair. It's not a whole lot to go off of, but it's something. We were able to stop our focus on certain suspects and put more effort into finding the correct ones. We'll find who did it. Until then, you two are free to go back to Boston if you wish, but it is possible we might need you to come back at some point. We'll keep you updated."

Swallowing is difficult. I nod my head as I try to keep the bile down.

"Thank you," I manage to get out before grabbing my crutches and racing for the exit. Finn catches up just in time to open the door for me. I bolt out and go as fast as my broken ankle will allow.

"Slow down. Hey! Daphne!" He softly grabs my elbow and holds me in place as he puts his body in front of mine. "What is it?"

"I know who did it." Tears immediately stream down my face. "I know who fucking did it."

"Who?" he demands, his face rigid.

"I'm not telling you."

"WHAT?" he yells.

"Bring me home. I want to go home right now."

I twist my arm out of his grasp and ignore the pain of my foot as I hop into the Wrangler by myself and shut the door. Finn immediately gets in, too, but doesn't start the engine. I know he isn't going to give up on this easily so I'm going to have to tell him, but only if he gives me his word.

"Promise me. Promise me if I tell you, you're just going to keep your mouth shut and let this be over. If you can't do that, I can't tell you. I never will."

"I don't like this. Someone tried to fuckin' burn you alive. Why the hell would you want to protect that person?"

"Because she gave me life." My chest heaves, and the air becomes thick.

"No way," Finn shakes his head. "There's no way a mother could do that to her child. What makes you think it was her?"

"Jarrod's sweatshirt. She emptied his house before I got there. The sweatshirt the detective described…it was Jarrod's."

Finn covers his face with his hands and leans over the steering wheel. "God dammit!" he yells, then looks at me. "Why? Why are you going to protect her after she treated you so horribly your entire life?"

"Because, no matter what, she's still my mother, and I can't do it to my dad. I just can't."

"So what am I supposed to do? Forget it ever happened? The vision of you hurt with fire all around you is forever etched into my brain. I see it every minute. What do you want me to do?"

"Take me home," I whisper as sobs escape me. "I'm so tired of being sad and crying. I want it to be over. Take me home so I can just be happy with you."

The soothing heat from Finn's hand cups my face as his thumb wipes away the tears from my cheek. Then he starts the engine and we drive in silence to the hotel.

Thankful to be resting on the bed for a little while in the hotel room, Finn adjusts my leg so my ankle is resting on a pillow. The pain has been awful all day, but now it's almost agonizing. Still not enough for me to take a pain pill. I'm trying to wait to take that until we are driving home so I can sleep during the trip.

"I have some business to take care of, but I feel like I can't trust you to stay here," Finn says, sounding frustrated.

"You can't tell the police, Finn. I'm begging you." My hands reach for him and desperately hold onto the black fabric of his sleeveless shirt.

"You trusted me with that, I'm not going to the police. There are a few things to straighten out with Ryan, though. Will you promise me to stay here? When I get back, we'll go home if you're feeling up to it."

I relax back into the bed knowing he's going to Ryan's and not to the police. "I'll stay here."

He hands me the remote, gives me a kiss, and heads out.

Finn is gone for a few hours. I'm not able to fall asleep like I had hoped and my ankle is throbbing, but I'm saving my pain pill for the ride back to Boston. All I can think about is getting home and lying in my own bed, far away from here. So, as soon as he walks into the door, he gathers our things and takes me away from the city that has caused me so much pain.

* * *

I YAWN AND BLINK RAPIDLY, allowing my eyes to adjust to the light. The bed is empty next to me and then, confusion takes over. I forget about my ankle and use my feet to push me up to a sitting position in the bed. I suck in air, making a hissing sound out of pain. Finn comes bolting into the room.

"You okay?"

"Yeah, just moved it wrong."

"That pain pill must have really knocked me out last night. I don't even remember the drive or getting home."

Finn chuckles. "Tell me about it. I carried dead weight from the parking garage all the way up to your apartment. You didn't wake up once all night."

Just being in my apartment already has me feeling much better.

"I made you a doctor's appointment for later this afternoon. As much as I want to take you, there's somethin' at the pub I gotta take care of."

"Is everything okay?" I ask.

Finn flashes his inside melting smirk at me. "It's fine. Nothing serious. Leigh is going to take you. Figured you wouldn't mind."

"Shit."

"What's wrong now?"

"I need a shower. How the hell am I supposed to manage that?"

Finn's expression radiates excitement as his eyes scan over my body. "I'll help you."

"I bet you will," I laugh.

He scoops me up, and I squeal as he hustles to the bathroom.

"I thought you had to get to the pub?"

"I'm gonna be late."

* * *

"Can we get burgers?" I ask Leigh. We're halfway home from the doctor's office and my stomach is growling.

"Um...I..."

"Don't tell me you aren't hungry. I wouldn't believe it."

She laughs but before she can say anything her phone rings.

"Yeah? Okay, no problem." Ending the call, she turns to me. "Finn wants me to bring you to the pub. He wants to see your cast."

"I swear, that man doesn't even trust a doctor with me."

"He loves you," Leigh reminds me, and I nod.

Pulling up to the pub, it looks like there's no power inside. Leigh and I walk to the door and see a handwritten sign taped to the window.

CLOSED TODAY. WILL REOPEN AT 11AM TOMORROW.

"What the hell? This pub has never closed."

Leigh pulls open the door, and I cautiously step inside. I see a little light coming from the back office.

"Finn?" I call. There's no way I'm going to try to navigate through the tables with these crutches when I can't see.

With the sound of a switch, light replaces the dark, and my breath is stolen from within me. In order to stop the audible gasp from coming out of my mouth, my hand covers it as tears form in the corners of my eyes. Daffodils. Bright, yellow, happy daffodils. Everywhere. An entire line of vases filled with bouquets of yellow run from one end of the bar to the other. Even more vases sit on each table. Movement from the back catches my attention, and I watch Finn strut slowly toward me. The closer he gets, the faster my heart beats until he stops right in front of me.

"Finn?" I whisper.

"I've been in love with you, since the day you stepped foot into this pub. Love I didn't think was ever possible. Even the thought of almost losin' that is excruciating. I never want to be one day without you."

"Finn, what are you saying?"

"I'm sayin' it's time for a new beginning, Daffodil."

Without losing eye contact, he grabs my hand and his body begins to lower to the ground. My mouth drops open even further on a gasp.

"Be my wife. Will you marry me?"

Blinking rapidly to release the tears that built up, I try to find words. Any words.

"I can't," I breathe.

CHAPTER SIXTEEN

FINN'S SMILE FALLS, and his eyes look to me, concerned. I know I need to say something quickly.

"There's a strict policy discouraging relationships among employees," I say.

Finn's dimple reappears on his face as he chuckles.

Kael pops up from behind the bar and startles me. "Daphne, you're fired."

Suddenly, the pub fills with whispered giggles, and I laugh.

"Yes. Yes I'll marry you."

Finn springs from the floor, wrapping his arms around my waist, causing my crutches to fall, and swings me around. As our lips touch, there's a rush of clapping and cheering as people start popping out from places around the bar. Tenderly, he sets me onto a chair and slides the perfect cushion cut canary yellow diamond on my left ring finger. Who knew how much I would grow to love yellow.

Leigh rushes to me, pulling me into a tight hug. "I knew all day long," she whispers in my ear. Of course she did.

Kael, Tasha, Sophie, Benson, and Paul all take their turn congratulating us with embraces. A few minutes go by before I look around the room and it dawns on me.

"Did you seriously close the pub?" I ask Kael.

He nods, "It's reserved for a private party."

The guys pull the scattered tables together to make one long one down the center of the pub. Finn settles me in the chair on the end with another chair off to the side for my leg to rest on since it's supposed to be elevated as much as possible. Watching him interact with all of his friends and family, the smile doesn't leave his face. He looks so happy, and soon, I realize my lips have also been in a constant upright position.

"Mom, Finn has something to tell you," Kael says into his phone before handing it to Finn.

"She said yes." He smirks while looking in my direction while talking to his mother. "Yes, I'll keep you updated. Love you, too."

I can't help but smile a little harder knowing Siobhan knew her son was planning to propose.

Waiters I've never seen before start bringing in plates of food from the kitchen. I watch as they set down beautiful steaks in front of everyone. Then I see what was put in front of me. A huge bowl of cinnamon and sugar squares. I burst out in laughter.

"You said it was your favorite," he jokes. Then a waiter comes to my side and removes the bowl of cereal and replaces it with the same dinner as everyone else.

"Wait! Are you throwing that away?" I ask, still laughing.

"There's no milk in it. You can eat it later." Finn's mischievous grin comes closer and kisses me.

"Wait. I don't want to lose my job. I love working here," I say, suddenly remembering what Kael said. I hope he was kidding.

"You're fired from your waitress position. You'll have a new one here as an O'Reilly. Co-owner," he says, smiling from ear to ear.

When dinner is finished Kael starts spitting out drinks at the bar and cranks the music. Finn constantly checks on me and has forbid me from getting out of the chair. I watch him happily chat with Leigh in the corner.

"You okay?" Paul asks as he pulls up a chair next to me. He looks dapper in his usual black dress pants with a tucked in black button-up dress shirt. The three buttons on the top are undone, the sleeves folded up.

"I am. Thanks."

"I know if it were my woman in danger, I'd want to know everything so I could protect her." His eyes zone in on the floor between us. He quickly shakes his head then turns to me. "I hope you aren't angry that I dug into Ryan. I was just trying to help Finn."

"I'm not. I know you were trying to help. It's okay." I smile and place my hand on his forearm. His smile back makes my heart ache. Paul seems like such a sweet man, but the darkness lurking inside of him emits from his pores. I should mind my own business, but I just can't.

"Maybe this is overstepping, but if you ever want to talk about anything, you can talk to me. Sometimes talking to someone who is outside of the circle and unbiased can help."

"Who said you were outside of the circle?" he snickers. "You're marrying one of my best friends. You couldn't be more in the circle."

I don't think my heart could be fuller than it is at this moment. "You know what I mean. I'm in here every Wednesday night, I see you."

Paul gives a knowing nod. "Maybe one day I'll take you up on that." He places a caring hand on my shoulder, gives me a warm smile, then rises from the chair. "You ever need anything, I'm a phone call away."

He smiles, then he walks away from the table and over to where Kael and Finn are leaning against the bar.

Sophie, Tasha, and Leigh scoot down the table from where they were sitting, and all take seats around me.

"I'm so sorry about your brother's house," Sophie says. There's that word again, but surprisingly, it doesn't make my skin crawl like it did right after Jarrod died.

"Let me see that rock," Leigh shrieks, saving me from having to talk anymore about the fire. She grabs my hand and gasps.

"Oh, it's lovely." she says.

It really is gorgeous. I've never been a big fan of jewelry. But this ring was made for me to wear. The diamond in the center isn't obnoxious, and it is surrounded by a dozen or so tiny diamonds all set in white gold.

"It is gorgeous," Tasha kicks in.

"When I saw the look on your face when he was holding his niece, I knew it was only a matter of time," Sophie says, smiling before she takes a sip from her glass.

I look to the bar and see the bottles of wine that are open, then look back to Sophie's glass.

"There's an awful lot of bubbles in your glass to be wine," I say, leaning into her with one of my eyebrows raised.

Her face turns fire engine red, and the widest smile beams across her face.

"It's ginger ale. I just found out. I'm telling Benson tonight," she bursts with excitement.

We all squeal around her as she laughs. Every man in the pub moves in our direction, concern on their faces, until they see us giggling. As they approach, we clear our throats and try to stifle the giddiness we all feel about Sophie being pregnant.

"You ready to go home, Sweets?" Benson asks her.

"I am," she replies, giving us all her sneaky smile.

Paul leaves the same time Benson and Sophie do. Kael and Tasha are in the back cleaning up and getting the pub ready for tomorrow. And Finn has joined me at the table.

"Are you happy?" he asks me.

"Beyond," I breathe.

His muscles contract as he leans over the corner of the table and kisses my lips. The warmth of his breath travels across my cheek and chills leap up my spine as he whispers into my ear.

"I can make you happier. At home." Then his tongue touches my earlobe. "Let's go."

* * *

GOOSEBUMPS RISE on my skin as Finn teases my upper thigh with his fingertips the entire drive to my apartment. Clambering up the stairs to the door of the building only lasts for a second before Finn lifts me off my feet and hauls me all the way up to my door. Digging in my purse, I find my key and open the door. Herman comes meowing, but Finn doesn't put me down.

"You'll have to wait, cat."

I laugh as he charges straight for the bedroom and places me on the bed. His hands travel the length of my legs until they touch my black lace panties. This morning I put on a dark gray summer dress so it would be easy with the cast at the doctor's office. By the look on Finn's face, it's made this real easy, too. He takes his time sliding the lace down my legs and tosses it to the floor. My body shivers as fingertips trace up my sides, pulling the dress with them. As he lifts it over my head, he licks my neck from the collarbone up to my jaw, and chuckles as my body shivers again.

"You okay?"

"So much better than okay," I whisper.

The grin on his face gets wide, and before he lowers himself to me, I grip the back of his head. Our lips touch and his need for me is obvious on my thigh. I grasp him through his pants as our bodies continue to move and sway together. A hiss comes from his mouth and quickly repays me with his fingers. Fumbling, I undo his zipper and push them down as far I can reach without moving my leg. He kicks off his shoes, then steps right out of them.

His tongue drags across my lower abdomen to my hip where he places a kiss. A palm rests on one of my breasts while I feel the heat from his mouth just above my other nipple. The room stills, and Finn's movements cease. I wait, and just as I'm about to open my eyes to see why he stopped, his mouth closes around my nipple and a whimper escapes me. The movement of his body upward places him right at my wetness, and I move my hips, begging him to enter me.

"Are you mine?"

"Yes," I whisper.

"Say you're mine."

"I've been yours for years, and I'll be yours forever."

Finn angles his hips and lines himself up with my opening as he gently works his way in. My head tilts back as he fills me. His slow and steady movements don't last for long. His muscles are twitching, and I know he's holding back.

"Finn," I beg, pulling on his hips.

Holding himself above me, he sucks in his bottom lip. "Your leg," he whispers.

"I feel nothing but you," I pant. "Plea..."

I can't finish speaking as Finn thrusts into me. Our bodies move together in sync. He puts himself so deep, nothing could get us closer. A moan comes from deep within Finn as I begin to tremble around him. My moans echoing in my bedroom are soon joined by his guttural groans as he climaxes. Then he looks down, and flashes me that perfect side smile.

Finn climbs back into bed after cleaning himself and me. I try to curl into him but the heavy cast cuts is uncomfortable and I grunt out of frustration. Finn grabs one of the pillows behind his head and places it between his legs. Then he pulls me into him and positions my cast on the pillow.

"How attached to this apartment are you?" he asks.

"A little. Why?"

"Benson pulled me aside at the pub tonight. There's a condo for sale in his building. He thinks it would be perfect for us."

"What about your condo? And Kael?"

"Kael loves that place enough to buy it. It all comes down to you. If you want to stay here, we can."

The thought of leaving this apartment is bittersweet. It was the first place away from Jarrod that felt like home to me. The first place that was actually mine. But a part of me is ready to move on with Finn.

"When can we go look at it?"

"In a few days. I have to work at the pub tomorrow. There's a lot of paperwork Kael fucked up while I was gone. I'll be there all day. Benson and Sophie are going back to the mountains this weekend so it will have to be before they leave."

Spotting the light-colored scar on Finn's chest, my fingers begin their soft journey over it. The sliver of light coming from the slit in the curtains I didn't fully close catches the diamond on my finger.

"So when do you want to do this?" I ask him sleepily as I hold up the stunning ring.

"As soon as you want to. Do you have any ideas about what kind of wedding you want?"

"No clue. I'm going to call Ally in the morning to see if she can help me plan it out. You did make everything better with Ryan right?"

"Yeah," he mutters.

"Is there anything in particular you want?"

"Not really. You can do whatever you want as long as you become my wife at the end."

"Anything you don't want?"

"Candles," he replies.

* * *

"NOTHING. Do you hear me? If you want food, order it. I'll clean whatever mess there may be later. You sit. Watch TV and keep that foot up." Finn tosses my pillow in the air a few times to fluff it before placing it behind my back on the couch. He pulls my blanket up to my chest and pets Herman, who has already climbed on top of me.

"Yeah, yeah," I mumble and roll my eyes.

"Love you," he says.

"I love you, too."

The minute the door closes behind him, I call Ryan.

"Hey, Daphs," Ryan greets.

"I've got some news."

"Good news, I hope. I'm not sure I can handle much more bad."

"Finn and I got engaged last night."

"That's great! I'm happy for you, Daphs."

"I'm going to call Ally to see if she has the time to help me. I have no idea what I'm doing with a wedding or how to plan one."

"Oh, she'll love that. She's in Boston now actually, meeting with a client she has there. I don't know if she has the time, but if she does, it wouldn't surprise me if she stopped by before coming back to Albany."

"I'll call her and see. That would be awesome."

"I'm just walking into a restaurant for a business meeting, so I have to go. Congratulations."

"Thanks. We'll talk again soon."

As soon as I hang up with Ryan, I call Ally. Her scream of excitement about makes me go deaf in one ear. She has to finish a few things up with her client and then she is bringing over a late lunch. While I wait for her, I plop back down like I promised and start scanning the Internet for wedding ideas on my laptop.

The buzzer sounding off in my apartment sends my body springing off the couch. I was sucked so far down the Internet hole that all sense of time vanished. I hobble over to the speaker and call down.

"Hello?"

"It's me, Daphne."

"C'mon up, Ally"

Usually, I would light all of my candles so that my apartment had a cozy smell to it. But since the fire, I think I'm going to get rid of them all. When Finn said he didn't want candles at our wedding, I knew exactly what he was talking about. He can't look at those flames any more than I can. Quickly, I race to straighten up the mess of blankets off the couch so that Ally has a place to sit. She knocks softly then walks in with bags of food.

"Roast beef?" Ally asks.

"Yum!"

She sets the bags on the kitchen counter, then turns and wraps her arms around me.

"Congratulations. You deserve this."

"I don't know about deserving it. But I'm happy."

"You wear happiness well," she says, standing back and looking me over. "Let's eat, I'm starving."

Ally carries all the bags from the kitchen into the living room and sets all of our food up on the coffee table.

"Do you have any ideas of a theme you might want for your wedding?" Her smile is as wide as her face.

"I have no clue, but I saw this dress online. What do you think?" I point to the beautiful dress on my open computer.

Suddenly, we both jump as Finn busts through the door of my apartment. He swings at my face and with brute force, knocks the cup I have out of my hands. The liquid goes spilling out all over my cream carpet.

"What the hell is wrong with you, Finn?"

"She did it," he says winded. "She fucking did it." His finger visibly shakes as he points it at Ally.

"You're not making any sense," I say. "What are you talking about?"

"The cops are looking for her. They have proof she set your brother's house on fire."

Air gets sucked into my lungs at such a rapid pace that it makes an awful gasping sound as I stand. "What?" I ask unbelieving.

He grabs ahold of my elbow and pulls me close to his side and far from Ally. "They also have proof that she was in Boston every time Ryan was. I'd bet money she roofied you on more than one occasion."

Ally's face grimaces. I'm almost positive that it was my mother. It doesn't make sense that Ally would do any of those things. Ally is my friend and Ryan's girlfriend. Why would she do that?

"How do you know this?" I ask.

Before Finn can answer, Paul comes running into my apartment, followed by the Boston PD.

"Allison Bertram, you're under arrest for suspected arson, attempted murder, and aggravated battery."

I can barely comprehend what is happening. The air in the room becomes heavy. Staring into her eyes, I don't believe it until her expression hardens and her face turns cold.

"How could you?" I whisper painfully.

"Ryan wanted me to move into that house. Do you know that? Where your brother hung himself, he wanted me to live there. He couldn't let go of Jarrod. He couldn't let go of you either." She speaks through the officer reading her Miranda Rights as he's trying to push her out of the apartment. "Every time he talks about you or hears your name, his eyes light up. Just once, he should have that reaction to *ME*. If I was going to be happy, I had to get rid of that house. And *you*." Her voice echoes in the hall as they push her out of my building.

My eyes widen, and breathing becomes difficult. Finn pulls me into his chest protectively as we watch the police gather evidence from the food and liquid that was in the cup I was about to drink from.

"I still don't get it. What was the point of the roofies?"

"My guess would be that she didn't trust you with Ryan so every time you were together, she knocked you out with the drug. Maybe worse," Paul says.

The cops dissect my apartment. They pull a container of crushed pills, a lighter, and a gas station gift card out of her bag.

"My next guess is, today she was about to plant that shit in your apartment to make you look guilty for setting the fire," Paul continues.

"Did you drink any of that or eat anything?" Finn asks me.

"I'm fine, and no. I was just about to, though. At least I know my mother wasn't trying to kill me," I say, trying to joke. "But how did you figure it out?"

"Paul wasn't convinced it was your mother."

"You told him?"

"I had to. He told me he wasn't stopping until he knew who almost killed you. I was trying to persuade him to stop by telling him it was your mother, but he didn't believe that."

"Wait. I thought you worked with Benson as a developer. What are you, a PI or something?" I ask him.

"Nope. I just know a lot of people. People who will do shit for me anytime I ask. Trust me, you don't want to know any more. I'm glad you're safe now. I'm going home to take a nap," Paul says nonchalantly. He smacks Finn's hand and brings him in for that man side hug they do, and then he walks out.

"I think I'm kind of done with this apartment," I say, looking around at the place that used to bring me peace.

Finn grabs his phone out of his pocket, dials a number, then holds it up to his ear.

"Knoxx. You busy? We want to come look at the apartment. Good. Yes, she's fine, and Ally is in custody. See you in an hour."

"How did anyone even know Ally was here? Did Paul have some creepy guy following me?"

"That wouldn't have fuckin' flown with me. You should know that. I called Ryan," he says.

"Oh my God. Ryan."

CHAPTER SEVENTEEN

"RYAN?" I call his name as I hear the line pick up.

"Daphs, thank God you're okay. Holy shit you have no idea what it's like right now for me to hear your voice."

"I'm so sorry."

I can't imagine how Ryan is feeling. He's lost his best friend, the house he wanted to buy, and now his longtime girlfriend.

"I should be the one who's sorry," he says. "She did all of it because of me. Damn, I would have never forgiven myself."

"What are you going to do now?"

"I'm on my way to you. Finn asked me to come."

"Really?"

I look to Finn, lowering the phone beneath my chin so that Ryan doesn't hear me. "You want Ryan here?"

"Yeah, I figured you could use him around for a bit."

I throw my arms around the man I love so much.

"We'll plan to see you for dinner then?"

"I'll be there."

* * *

AFTER A LONG AFTERNOON answering the police's questions and giving statements, we get into the Wrangler and head for Benson's building. The valet walks in front of the vehicle and nods at Finn while he takes his key from him. I'm not even sure how we can afford to live in such a fancy building. The money Gram gave me is decent, but I'm not sure it's this building's version of decent.

Walking into the lobby, Benson's tall frame is leaned against the counter. His eyes are angled down to his phone as he types viciously.

"Knoxx," Finn calls to him. Benson pushes off and rushes toward us. His welcoming white smile shines before he places a kiss on either side of my face. He turns to Finn, doing that same hand smack and side man hug that Finn and Paul exchanged earlier.

"Jesus, I'm glad that's over for you, Daphne," he says, shaking his head.

"Me too."

"Let's head on up and see if you like it."

Finn and I nod, then follow Benson to an elevator adjacent to the one that we used when we visited the Knoxx's. Once we get inside, I notice it has no floor numbers. Just a keypad and a passcode. Benson punches in a five-digit code, the doors close, and the elevator goes up. And up.

"Here we are," Benson says as the doors open and we're greeted by a foyer.

Eyes wide, I turn to Finn. "I don't think we can afford this."

"Let's just look at it and appease him."

As we walk across the foyer, we come to a heavy, dark wood, six-panel door. Benson opens it, and the sheer beauty of the place takes my breath away. This condo is quite different from Benson and Sophie's. Everything is dark and cozy. The walls are a deep greige color that runs throughout the space. Coming around the corner to the kitchen, it features rich dark wood cabinets with white marble counters and stainless appliances. The floors are a welcoming chestnut, and the space is accented with bright white trim. I fall more in love with the place as Benson shows us every room. I thought pulling up to this building that I would feel like I was betraying the girl I became. Coming to Boston, I was running away from the rich, uptight crowd my family grew up with. But this feels so different. No one looked at me strangely or like I didn't fit in here. I was comfortable just like I was in my tiny humble apartment.

"I'm going to run upstairs to chat with Sophie for a minute and let you two talk."

Once Benson leaves, I giggle toward Finn.

"I like it here," I say.

"Me too. Let's do it. Benson and I have already discussed price. I'm getting the family discount apparently, whether I agree or not," he chuckles. "He said if we like it, it's ours."

"Oh my God," I squeal and wrap my arms around him as he buries his head into my neck and places a soft kiss.

After signing paperwork with Benson, he tells us we can move in whenever we're ready. With all the drama that unfolded today, this is an amazing surprise. I'm exhausted though, and all I want to do right now is lie down and go to sleep. But as I clamber into Finn's Wrangler, my stomach growling reminds me that Ryan should be getting into town any time now.

"I should check in at the pub. Do you want to go to there with me? You can have Ryan meet us, and we can eat something there. It's up to you."

"That'll work. I need to call Leigh and ask her if she'll feed Herman. That's the only bad thing about leaving my apartment. I'm going to be sad to not have Leigh across the hall anymore for last-minute hangout sessions."

"I'm not trying to take you away from anything. I'll understand if you would rather stay in your apartment. If that's what you want, I'll move in with you."

Leave it to Finn to know exactly what to say to make me love him even more. But I know he likes Benson's condo and he wouldn't mind being closer to Sophie and Katie when they are in town.

"I want to move into the condo with you. Your condo is a bachelor pad and my apartment is small. We should start our lives somewhere new. A place that has no negative memories for me. The valet won't be torturous either," I snicker.

He reaches over and encloses my hand with his, lifting it and pressing his lips to it. Our hands remain joined on our ride to the pub. I take advantage of the time to call Leigh and fill her in on everything.

"Don't worry, I've got Herman taken care of. You relax and do whatever you need to. I can't wait to have mommy night out at your new condo. Just don't expect me to show up in anything other than my pajamas. Tradition is tradition."

I giggle, knowing damn well Leigh is never going to step foot out in public in pajama pants. I'm pretty sure she's never even worn yoga pants outside of our building.

"We'll have to make it a weekly date. I'll even have a spare room to keep some toys for Landon so he can come, too."

"He'll love that. Did you and Finn talk about a date yet? Oh! Should I not talk about the wedding after what happened this morning?"

"We haven't talked about it. I was excited until that crazy bitch came over. I was certain it was my mother. As if I didn't have enough issues with her."

"I don't even know what to say."

"It's over. Let's not talk about it anymore. I'll let you know as soon as Finn and I figure things out. Thanks for taking care of Herman."

"You are very welcome."

Right after I end the call with Leigh, I send Ryan a text to meet us at the pub. He said on the phone he was doing okay, but I'm not sure I believe him.

When Ryan finally walks into the pub, he makes a beeline in my direction and wraps his arms around me. After a minute, we slide into a booth and order some drinks.

"You might want to scoot all the way toward the wall," I tell Ryan.
"Why?"

"Tasha is our waitress. If she spills, hopefully it will be toward the end of the table," I laugh and Ryan does, too, which sets me at ease for his mood. He doesn't seem overly distraught like I was afraid he might.

"I've made a decision."

The way Ryan made the declaration has me a little nervous. Hopefully, he isn't making rash decisions in light of what Ally has done.

"Let's hear it."

"I'm moving to New York. I'm always there on business and I've always loved the city. With Ally, Jarrod, and the house gone, maybe this is my opportunity to start fresh somewhere new." His expression falls. "But I made a promise to Jarrod. One I don't intend on breaking. So if you say you need me here, I won't—"

"Go."

"Daphs, are you sure? You've been through—"

"I'm fine. It's not like you're moving to Mars. Just a little extra time in the car. And Lord knows you'll be calling me." I shoot him a smile, and the tension eases out of his shoulders. "It's time we both start making ourselves a priority. I'd offer to help you move, but you'll have to wait for a million years to pass before I get this stupid ass cast off of my foot first."

"It'll be off before you know it. Time goes by so fast. To think it's already been so long since Jarrod passed."

Finn walks up to our booth. He holds out his hand to shake Ryan's, then climbs in next to me.

"Oh *shit*," Tasha cries as the tray she's carrying begins to teeter on her hand. A little soda spills over the side and right onto Finn's arm on the table. "I'm so sorry, Finn," she says, with fear in her eyes.

Ryan and I look at each other and burst out laughing.

"It's okay, Tasha. You're getting better though," I say, trying to save her.

"Thanks," she says, ignoring the fact that Finn's arm is soaked. "Kael has been helping me with my balance."

"Oh, he has?" I say, interested.

"Yeah the other night—"

She's interrupted by Finn clearing his throat. "Can I have some napkins, please?" he asks, trying to hold in his grin but failing.

She blushes and sets down our drinks, then rushes off to grab some napkins from the bar.

"So when are the two of you getting married? Have you thought about a date?" Ryan asks, looking at both of us.

"We haven't had time to talk about it. I was going to ask Ally how long the planning usually takes, but we all know how that went," I say.

"I think the average is about a year, but Ally had to plan a wedding in just a few days before," Ryan chimes in, then takes a drink of his stout.

A year seems like an eternity. Ryan's right. Time goes way too fast, and I don't want to waste a minute of it. Marrying Finn will be one of the best days of my life, and life is so short.

"Why don't you see when your parents can come again? As soon as they can get here. That's when we'll get married. I don't need anything special. Just our family, friends, a dress, and you," I say, smiling to Finn.

Finn stands from the booth and begins to walk away.

"Hey? Where are you going?"

"To call my parents. Let's see just how fast they can get here." The sexy glare he shoots me paired with the side grin sends shivers down my spine.

"I'd marry that man right here and now."

I don't realize that I said those words out loud until my head turns forward again to see Ryan smiling.

"It's real good to see you happy, Daphs. It's about damn time."

* * *

IT'S BEEN three weeks since Ally was arrested in my living room. She was in possession of a gas gift card that was used at the gas station around the corner from Jarrod's house. In a box in the back of her closet, they found Jarrod's sweatshirt that Ryan admitted to taking from the house in remembrance of his best friend and a few Rohypol pills. She's pretty screwed.

Ryan packed up all of his belongings from her house and rented an apartment in New York City. And he thought my apartment was small.

Leigh has been driving me crazy about the wedding. I swear she is more excited than I am, and I'm pretty damn excited. She's been over every day with Landon, helping me pack up my apartment to get ready for our move into the new condo along the Harbor. My favorite time is when we snuggle up on the couch and look at all the pretty wedding stuff. She picks out pale pinks, and I pick out dark greys. We mostly laugh at our differences. She didn't laugh when I showed her the picture of the wedding dress I ordered. She teared up and hugged me tightly, saying it was perfect and that she'll take me for all the fittings.

Finn and I decided to keep our wedding simple. We're getting married at my favorite place on the Riverwalk along the water. Then we'll go back to O'Reilly's for a small get-together before going to our new home together for the first time. I've never looked forward to something so much in my entire life. We set the date for six weeks from the day he proposed. Right when I get my cast off. I'm not walking down the aisle in my wedding dress with two crutches. Now I'm just counting down the days.

"What about this?" Leigh asks as she holds up a black tunic sweater that I haven't worn in at least a year.

"Donate."

She throws the sweater in the growing pile of things going to Goodwill. Landon is running around like a mad man on a sugar rush. Finn took him for ice cream today after lunch.

"So who is going to walk you down the aisle?" Leigh asks, but I can tell by her face that she regrets the words coming out of her mouth the minute the last syllable left it. She knows I haven't been able to get ahold of my daddy since I spoke to him in the hotel room. "I'm sorry. I know that's a touchy subject."

"It's okay. I'm going to walk alone. Lots of brides do it. So can I." I stick my nose far into the air to show my confidence, and Leigh puts up her hand as we giggle and high-five like teenagers. "Have you found a bridesmaid dress you like yet?"

"I still think we should all be matching. I feel weird picking out a different style dress than everyone else."

"That's the whole point. You each get to pick what you are comfortable in. It just has to be the same gray color, but you need an extra ribbon or something."

Leigh cried when I asked her to be my matron of honor. I couldn't imagine anyone else standing next to me. Sophie and Tasha are bridesmaids. Landon is our ring bearer and, of course, Katie is our flower girl. I couldn't be surrounded by more loving people on the day I marry Finn. Benson, Kael, Paul, and Finn already have their tuxedos.

"So what's left?" Leigh asks me, adding more candles she found into the donation box.

"We have to choose a cake, find an ordained minister, and decide what we are doing for dinner back at the pub. Oh, and I have to order the flowers. How am I ever going to get all of that done in just three weeks?"

"It's not just you anymore. You have a group of people around you that are willing to help you do anything. Besides, if someone doesn't produce, I'm sure Paul has a guy for that," Leigh says as we both laugh again. Truth is, I'm sure he actually does.

* * *

"Can I help you?"

Leigh and I have barely stepped foot into the bridal shop when a petite older woman races in our direction.

"I got a call that my dress order is in?"

Her excited expression fades. "Okay. This way."

She leads us into the back to the fitting rooms. In the middle of all of the rooms is a white step that is surrounded by a half circle of mirrors. Just behind that is a bench for your guests to view the dress as well. My palms get sweaty as I hobble with my crutches into the fitting room where my dress is still concealed in a bag.

"Do you want me to come in there and help you?" Leigh asks.

"No, I want to see your face when you see it for the first time. That will tell me everything I need to know."

It takes me a while and a few "Are you okay?" questions from Leigh, but I manage to get the dress on fine. It fits almost perfectly and hopefully it will just need a few little stitches here and there. The door creaks as I open it as slowly as I can in order to capture Leigh's entire face. Yep. I was right. It said all I needed to know.

"You can close your mouth, Leigh," I giggle as the saleswoman helps me hobble up onto the step.

"Absolutely stunning. You're going to melt that poor man right where he stands when he sees you in that."

Accompanying a huge grin are tears running down her cheeks. Before I know it, my face is wet, too. There's been no doubt that Leigh and I are close, but it's so much more than that. She's like my family. The female companion and role model I've never had. I turn to the mirror, and stare at the reflection. Never in my wildest dreams did I think this moment would ever come. But here I am.

* * *

"THAT'S DISGUSTING," Finn chokes. "You make me wait for an hour with only a wall between me and you in that dress, only to come here after and make me try lemon cake? I'm thinkin' Elvis marryin' us is soundin' better and better."

Finn was not amused that he had to wait outside while I had my appointment with the seamstress for my dress. He keeps asking me what it looks like and I refuse to tell him anything.

"Here, try this one," I say, laughing at his pouting face.

"No way. I don't trust your taste buds anymore."

"Finn, just try it."

"What is it?"

"Almond."

"What the ever lovin' hell are you tryin' to feed me? I'm done. I vote for chocolate. Just chocolate."

"You didn't even try the chocolate," I bark at him.

"Does it taste like chocolate?"

I take a bite out of the chocolate one, and its cocoa goodness fills my mouth.

"Yep."

"See? Easy. Simple. Why you women go all bonkers on weddings, I'll never understand. It's one day. All that matters is that we leave with you havin' the same last name as me."

I look to the baker who has been sitting with us throughout the cake debacle, and she has her hand over her face, trying to conceal her giggles. I just roll my eyes in defeat.

"We'll go with the chocolate," I say as Finn slowly leans in and kisses my cheek. I can almost feel that damned dimple on my face.

CHAPTER EIGHTEEN

NOT BEING able to work these past six weeks has been driving me nuts. Finn won't let me anywhere near a serving tray until I'm fully healed. Even though Kael tried to "fire" me from my position, I'm still looking forward to going back to bartend. But for now, I'm stuck in the apartment watching old reruns. The only good thing about it is having so much cuddling time with Herman. He loves me being at home and spends all evening with me on the couch. Leigh has been coming over to hang out. She usually laughs at me trying to bring my bowl of cereal to the couch. I usually can't make it without spilling some on the floor because of my stupid hobble.

With the cake, flowers, and food finished, there isn't much left to be done. My dress is altered and fits me perfectly. I gave Finn the job of finding someone to marry us. He assured me it's taken care of but I have no idea who he booked. I guess I'll find out at the wedding.

The buzzer sounds and I get to the speaker as quickly as I can.

"Hello?"

"It's Sophie!"

"C'mon up."

With the wedding only two days away, Benson and Sophie are back in town. I'm looking forward to spending some time with Sophie again. A few soft knocks on the door and it opens with her shinning smile.

"Wow, it's empty in here," she says as she looks around the almost bare apartment. We've been taking everything we want to keep over to the new condo. The only things left in the apartment are my bed, the couch, TV, and dishes. None of it we need in the new condo, so we'll be donating it after the wedding.

"I'm so excited to move. This apartment gave me what I needed when I needed it. Now I'm looking forward to something new."

She sets her white leather purse down and sits next to me on the couch.

"We need to talk about tomorrow."

"Tomorrow? I get my cast off tomorrow."

"No, I'm talking about tomorrow night. What do you want to do?"

"I haven't given it much thought."

"Why don't we rent a fancy hotel room and all the girls can stay with us? Then we'll all get ready there."

"That sounds like a lot of fun. I'll call—"

As I'm reaching for my cellphone, I get cut off by Sophie's voice on the phone with the hotel. She booked the largest suite they had and paid with her card.

"Sophie, you didn't have to do that."

"I know. I haven't always been able to do things for other people. Now that I'm able to, I like to do it. Especially for someone who's about to become family."

"Thank you. Speaking of family, I never asked how Benson reacted when you told him you were pregnant."

"He pointed to a chair and made me sit. Every time I've tried to do something, like carry in the groceries, he flips out and tells me to sit and relax. He's so damn bossy," she laughs while rolling her eyes. "What did you two end up deciding for dinner at the pub?"

"Sticking with the pub theme and trying to make this wedding true to our style, we're going with a slider bar and a potato bar. At the slider bar, you put together your own slider burgers and at the potato bar, you can choose from French fries, homemade potato chips, or potato wedges," I say, excited.

Sophie laughs "That is so you two. I'm looking forward to it."

Sophie and I share laugh after laugh as the night goes on. My stomach gets tighter with every passing minute as the wedding nerves continue to build. I don't doubt my love for Finn, but I'm still nervous. And I'd be lying if a small part of me doesn't wish my mom and dad were there. A big part of me wishes Jarrod would be there. My heart breaks again thinking about all the milestones in my life he won't be here for.

"Hey. You okay?" Sophie asks, placing her hand on my forearm.

"Yeah. I'm fine."

I shake my head to come back to the happiness that surrounds me. The excitement of what's to come and all of the amazing people that are being brought into my life.

"I'm going to get going. You should get some rest. How exciting to get your cast off. I bet you are so ready," she says as she stands and slowly walks toward her purse sitting by the door.

"I am. It's been a constant reminder of the fire, and I think we would all just like to forget about that."

She nods with a knowing smile. "I'll see you tomorrow night." Then she disappears out the door. Sophie is about as genuine as they come, and in a way, she reminds me so much of Leigh. Both of them have hearts bigger than the chest that holds them. I watch TV until Finn comes over after working at the pub. He scoops me up easily in his arms and takes me to bed. He can't wait for me to get my cast off either. His back has suffered since it gets hard for me to hold it up when he's on top of me.

* * *

"There. How does that feel?" Finn asks as he helps me into the Wrangler after getting my cast off.

"It's stiffer than I thought it would be, and it feels weak. What if I get wobbly trying to walk down the aisle?"

"You'll be fine. I can guarantee you, not one person at that wedding would let you fall. It will feel better once you take a shower. I'll help you," Finn says with a devilish grin.

With all the commotion about the wedding and getting my cast off, I forgot to tell Finn about the shindig Sophie planned with the girls tonight.

"I'm not going to be home tonight."

"What?"

"Sophie got a hotel for all the girls to stay at tonight. And you have to go with Benson and the boys. I'll see you tomorrow at the wedding."

"All of you girls in a hotel room? Alone?"

"We aren't teenagers, Finn," I scold him. "All the bad shit is behind us. I think us women are fully capable of staying the night in a hotel room."

Finn's pouty expression in the Wrangler all the way to my apartment building makes me laugh. He parks on the street next to my building, and I lean over the seat and place a kiss on his cheek.

"The next time you'll see me, it will be to make me your wife."

"Want me to walk you up?" he asks, grinning.

"Nope. I have to practice walking again. I'll take it slow. Leigh will be over soon."

Finn gets out and comes to my side, opening my door for me. He places a gentle hand on my elbow and eases me out. I wrap my arms around his waist and place my head on his chest. It doesn't take long before I feel his lips touch the top of my head as he squeezes my body.

"I love you, Daffodil."

"Love you, too."

Once I reach the corner of my building, I look back to see Finn watching and waiting to leave until I'm completely out of view.

It only takes about ten minutes after I walked into my door before Leigh's signature knock comes. Three knocks, then a pause, followed by two more, and she comes bouncing in.

"Whoo hooo! I'm off mom duty and you're getting married tomorrow. I'm so excited." She jumps onto the couch next to me.

"I'm going to miss the hell out of that knock," I say bummed.

"Me too. But that's not what we're focusing on right now. You are about to marry the man of your dreams, and we are going to celebrate. Now stop dillydallying and get ready."

Leigh's command has me smiling and hopping to action. I put on a pair of white skinny jeans with a black flowy top and sport my signature bouffant ponytail.

"Which ones?" I ask Leigh, holding up a pair of heels and a pair of flats.

"The flats. If you fall tonight, you'll be sorry tomorrow, and Finn will have our heads."

"Right," I agree as I slip the black flats on and grab my purse. "I'm ready. We just have to grab the dress and make sure we have everything for tomorrow."

Leigh and I pack everything we need into her car, and it looks like we are going on a trip for a month.

Pulling up to Amadeo's, I remember the last time I was here. It was the beginning of my friendship with Ally. Well, fake friendship rather. She was so good at keeping her hatred hidden. Just like the saying, she kept me closer. Now she'll regret it for the rest of her life.

"Daphne," Leigh calls from next to me. She had turned the car off, walked to my side, and opened the door. I hadn't noticed a thing.

"Geez. You were a million miles away. You all right?" Her worried eyes search mine.

"The last time I was here was with Finn, Ryan, and Ally."

"Shit," Leigh says quietly as she reaches for her phone.

Any time she cusses it makes me laugh, and this time is no different. I burst out laughing, but she isn't even cracking a smile.

"What are you doing?" I ask.

"I'm texting Sophie and Tasha. We'll eat somewhere else."

"No." I place my hand on Leigh's forearm and she looks up from her phone. "Replace bad memories with great ones." I stick my chin up in the air strongly, and Leigh grins.

"You've got it," she says, and we walk into the restaurant with linked arms.

. . .

WE COMPLETELY STUFF ourselves with appetizers, entrees, and drinks. I'm sure this is on some major list of things you shouldn't do the night before your wedding. I'm not one for following the rules anyway.

"What do you want to do tonight?" Tasha asks, leaning back in the booth with her hands on her belly. She looks miserably full.

"Yeah, we'll do whatever you want to. Maybe hit a few bars?" Leigh suggests.

"I feel horrible that I didn't have the entire night planned out. But with everything that has been going on lately, I just wasn't sure if you would be up to it," Sophie says.

"Will you call me a boring bitch if all I want to do is go back to the hotel, get the hell out of these tight pants, and hang out?"

In unison, all three girls shout, "No!" We laugh all the way out of the restaurant.

It's not even nine at night, and here we are. Four women in our pajamas in a fancy hotel, sprawled out all over the floor in front of the TV. Wine glasses, cupcake wrappers, blankets and pillows are everywhere. Our faces are covered in a thick gray mud mask as we watch a scary movie. The girls had gifted me with a beautiful satin white robe that says BRIDE on the back in light blue for me to wear tomorrow before I put my dress on. It brought tears to my eyes. For the first time, I have my own squad.

* * *

"DAPHNE, YOU LOOK STUNNING," Leigh says.

"Hair and makeup were here for hours, they better have done something," I joke back. "You all look so pretty."

Leigh, Sophie, and Tasha all look so beautiful in their dark gray dresses. I have on my corset and the robe the girls gave me last night. Clearing my throat of nerves, I walk over to the dress bag that is hanging from the closet door and slowly pull the zipper down. They gather around me as I guide the dress out of the bag. Leigh grabs one side, Sophie grabs the other, and they carefully lower it to the floor for me to step into. As they slide the dress up, Tasha removes my robe, then grabs onto the dress as Leigh moves to the back to take her place. Sophie and Tasha follow her to my back and watch her begin to button the dress up.

"Can I do that?" The small, frail voice has me spinning around. My mouth falls open.

"Mom?"

CHAPTER NINETEEN

"CAN I TALK TO YOU? ALONE?" she asks.

"If you are planning on ruining this day—"

"I would never do that."

I turn to Sophie, Leigh, and Tasha to see that they have moved in close to my back protectively.

"Can you give us a minute?" I ask them. "It's okay."

They nod and walk out of the room, leaving me standing there with my mother.

"What are you doing here?" I ask her.

"I couldn't bring myself to miss this."

"I thought I was dead to you," I say, crossing my arms over my chest. "Remember? Right after I lost everything, my own mother told me I was dead to her."

"I know there's a lot to explain. I should have done it before today. But if you'll let me, I'd really like to try."

Loudly sighing, I walk over to a chair by the window and sit, the back of my dress still undone. She doesn't sit and instead begins to rub her fingers together viciously. Although she looks especially put together in her fancy gray sequined dress, it's obvious how nervous she is.

"When Jarrod was born, things were tough. So tough that I just lost control. That's when we hired the first nanny. We never had planned to have another baby. You were an accident."

As the words leave her mouth, they slice through me. I knew it. She was here to say something awful to me on my wedding day and ruin it all for me. I stand up, refusing to hear another hateful word, and begin my march toward the door.

"No! Wait. That's not how it sounds." She takes a deep audible breath and sits on the edge of one of the beds. Her face is distraught and pained. "Please," she says as her shaky hand gestures back to the chair.

I make the choice to sit back down and listen to what she has to say.

"I knew what was already done to Jarrod. It killed me to think that I could do it to you, too."

"Do what?" I snap. "You seem to be dancing around, and right now, I don't understand. I have somewhere to be, so if you don't mind, get to what you're trying to say."

"I was told that children could develop mental illness from a mentally ill parent. I saw it in Jarrod. The first little black hole of sadness in his eye... I knew it was my fault. My illness caused his. I refused to let it happen to you. No matter how much it broke me, I couldn't let it break you. From the day you were born, you were strong and tenacious. You were different. So, I chose to push you away from me. I couldn't bring you down like I did your poor brother."

All the air has left my lungs.

"So my entire life I thought you hated me, and you thought you were protecting me? From you?" I whisper, unable to find a stable voice.

She nods and wipes the tears from her lower lashes. "All the parties your dad said we were going to were a lie. We have a cabin outside of town. He would take me there when I was too depressed to see straight. When I wanted nothing more than to end the pain. He would take me to the cabin, and he never left my side. I forced him to separate himself from you, so that I would be as far from you as I could be."

"I don't even know what to say."

"I have to get this out," she says. "I was diagnosed with severe depression, obsessive-compulsive disorder, and mild delusional disorder. The last ten years I've slowly gotten better with medication and therapy. I'm not cured and may never be. It's not nearly as bad as it was though. I was still too afraid to come around you. You dealt with enough with your brother."

The tears turn into sobs. I never knew. How could I have never known my mother was going through this? I guess she was successful in her plan.

"What changed? Why are you coming to me now?" I ask.

"Finn."

My body stiffens. "Finn?"

"After the fire, he began calling us. He talked to Harrold many times before he put him on speaker and made me listen to him. After the initial conversation, I started accepting calls from Finn. He never pushed me. The conversation was always about you and the things you were doing. The closer it got to the wedding, the more he would encourage us to come. I told him I wasn't going to come, in fear I would create a bad memory on your day. He pleaded with us this morning, and here I am." She slaps her hands down on her lap after she wipes another tear away with a tissue. "I'm sorry, Daphne. If you want me to leave—"

Standing, I race to my mother who's lived a life of such pain, and I wrap my arms around her. Tears shed from both of our eyes as a feeling I never thought I would feel in my life happens. The sensation of my mother hugging me back. After living in the moment for a minute, I sit back on my good heel.

"Will you button me up, Mom?"

Even if it's temporary, the glee in her eyes shines as she eagerly nods her head and smiles.

"But first, I want to give you something." She places a small crystal star in my hand. The one that was missing from the window in Jarrod's house. "He once told me how much he loved those crystals hanging in his window. Said they made him happy. Thought you would want a little piece of him with you today as you walk down the aisle."

"Thank you," I manage to get out through my sobs.

"Let's get you ready, dear."

I quickly run to the door to tell the girls to come back in. As soon as Sophie lays her eyes on my face, she reaches for her phone and dials a number.

"We've had a bit of a situation, and I need you to come back to the hotel, like now. I'll pay you double. Good." She hangs up the phone and winks at me. "The makeup artist will be back in a jiffy."

"Thank you," I say as my shoulders relax.

We go back to where we were standing when my mother came in. Only this time, Leigh, Sophie, and Tasha are in the back while my mother buttons up my wedding dress.

The makeup artist is fast and my face looks just as it did before I cried it all off. The girls are in formation around the corner from the spot by the water so that Finn can't see us. The music begins, and the bridesmaids and groomsmen walk down the aisle. Just as I'm about to begin my walk, my dad comes walking up beside me.

"Did you think I'd let my only daughter walk down her wedding aisle alone?"

My voice cracks, "Hi, Daddy."

He kisses my cheek, then I take his elbow as he leads me toward the man of my dreams. Finn's eyes travel from top to bottom, taking in the sheath satin and lace white wedding dress. As his eyes meet mine and the sun shimmers off a tear on his cheek. My dad places my free hand in Finn's, and I hand Leigh my simple bouquet of bright yellow daffodils.

"You have no idea how much I love you," Finn whispers.

I look to my mom and dad sitting in the front row behind me holding hands. I look to Eoin, who has his arm draped around a smiling and tearful Siobhan. Finn brought all of these people here, for me.

"Oh, I think I do."

I'm the happiest I've ever been in my entire life. As I stare at the man who is about to become my husband, I realize it only takes one. Because one decision, one phone call, one word, can crumble your entire world, leaving you buried, heartbroken, and barely breathing. It just takes one person to pull you out of the rubble. Just one.

Read on for a sneak peek of Buried Hearts, In the Dark #3!

MORE BOOKS BY C.E. JOHNSON

In the Dark Series

Done (In the Dark, #1)

Just One (In the Dark, #2)

Buried Hearts (In the Dark, #3)

Standalone

Rain

BEFORE YOU GO!

Please consider leaving an honest review. Reviews help authors, but they also help readers like you discover new books. Thank you for reading.

For exclusive sneak peeks, teasers, and updates, come join my Facebook reading group!
CE's Reading Roses

ABOUT THE AUTHOR

C.E. Johnson is an author of contemporary romance as well as romantic suspense novels. When not writing until all hours of the night (with lots of late night coffee runs), she loves to read books that have a strong, protective male with a soft spot for his feisty heroine. She prefers stories that rip your heart out completely, then kindly place it back with a HEA.

She lives in a suburb of Chicago with her husband, two kids, and some spoiled, rotten animals.

Authorcejohnson.com

facebook.com/authorcejohnson

twitter.com/AuthorCEJohnson

instagram.com/authorcejohnson

goodreads.com/AuthorCEJohnson

BURIED HEARTS
(IN THE DARK SERIES, #3)

"Love will take you down faster than any bullet. You cry tonight. Tomorrow, you bury it."

JOLENE HAD her life planned out. Nursing school. Husband. House with a picket fence. She had all her boxes checked until her life flips upside down. Turns out, O'Reilly's Pub is the perfect place for a freshly unemployed, divorced woman who currently lives in her parent's old house to get stood up on her first attempt at dating again. She's giving up on love and that ridiculous dating app. However, that doesn't change the fact that she needs a date to her best friend's gala.

The last thing Paul wants to do is attend a gala with his first love, parading around as her fake boyfriend. With the memory of her heartbroken face still haunting him, even years later, he agrees to go, hoping this will make up for the pain he caused her.
The plan? Go to the gala, make her ex-husband hate himself, then let her go. But that plan blows up the minute he believes Jolene has a stalker. Paul will have to put his guilt behind him if he's going to keep her safe. He won't lose another person he cares about. Especially not the woman he never wanted to leave in the first place.

Available Now! ->Buried Hearts

Made in the USA
Monee, IL
10 May 2022

96149106R00135